The Urge

By
Elaine C. Wolfe

Lost Legends Publishing, llc

(765) 606-5342

https://lostlegendspublishing.us/

© 2022 by the Author, Elaine C. Wolfe

All rights reserved. No part of this publication may be reproduced, stored in a retrieval system or transmitted in any form or by any means, electronic, mechanical, photocopying, recording or otherwise without the prior permission of the publisher or in accordance with the provisions of the Copyright, Designs and Patents Act 1988 or under the terms of any license permitting limited copying issued by the Copyright Licensing Agency.

Printed in the United States of America.

ISBN: (print)   979-8-9861136-0-9

ISBN: (digital) 979-8-9861136-1-6

The Urge

By
Elaine C. Wolfe

Dedication

This book is dedicated to my son, Scott; my daughter, Leah; my daughter-in law, Audra; my son-in-law, Ricardo; and my three grandchildren, Cole, Tessa, and Joseba. This book would never have been possible without their support and love.

Acknowledgments

First, I wish to acknowledge my parents who always encouraged me to read and learn. They didn't have the opportunity to go to college during the Depression years, but they were determined that I would be able to have that luxury.

Second, I wish to acknowledge the many colleges and universities, especially Purdue University, in preparing me to be an award-winning science educator.

Third, I wish to acknowledge my children, Leah and Scott, for proof-reading this book chapter by chapter. Their suggestions and corrections enabled me to finally reach one of my life-long ambitions, to write a novel.

Fourth, I wish to acknowledge my grandchildren, for wanting me to finish this book and saying "Grandma, you have to finish it because I want to read it".

Fifth, I wish to acknowledge my friends, both artist and teacher ones, who were anxious to read what I was working on and encouraged me.

Sixth, I wish to acknowledge all my wonderful students over the years. They made my life full of joy and satisfaction. When I saw the "lights go on in their eyes", I knew why I had chosen the teaching profession as my life's work. Many of them have continued to stay in touch over decades and become some of my close and dear friends.

Seventh, I wish to acknowledge my friend, Marian Betts, as a fellow Indiana Wildlife Artist, author, and CEO of Lost Legends Publishing, LLC, who pushed me to write and publish this book. She told me "if I can, you can."

Lastly and primarily, I wish to acknowledge God who in his mercy has granted me a long life, good health, good family, good friends, and so many innumerable blessings that I can't mention them all here.

Chapter 1
The University Student

Carmen Báez was the last student to leave the Madrid University library that evening. Her studies in pharmacy were getting more difficult, but as a third-year student, she was able to visualize the end of her studies in another year, maybe a year-and-a-half, and then a comfortable income in her future employment. She knew every back street to her apartment, which she shared with three other students, and was anxious to get home to continue her studying. She hadn't eaten dinner yet. It wasn't her night to prepare dinner; and, she knew, according to the agreement among the roommates, that whoever had cooked dinner that evening had left her a plate to be heated up in the microwave. With a major test tomorrow, it would be a long night.

As she turned down the last alleyway, a block, and a half from the apartment, she realized the streetlight, which usually made this part of her journey home as bright as a sunny afternoon, wasn't lit tonight. Oh well, such is life. That lamp had been flickering off and on for

The Urge

the last three weeks. Evidently, it had finally stopped working. Must have been the bulb she thought. They'd have to call it in to the civil authorities or it would be years before it would be fixed.

She had looked up at the streetlight, but as her gaze came down, she was being approached by a man who was all bent over and clutching his left leg as though he were in considerable pain. As he came closer, he asked her about the directions to the nearest hospital stating that a dog had bitten him, and he needed some medical attention. As if on cue, a dog barked in the distance. Carmen, wanting to be helpful, dropped her book bag and walked up close to the man to give him specific directions when he grabbed her. With one hand over her mouth and another around her waist, he pulled her into the deepest and darkest part of the alleyway behind the neighborhood recycling and trash bins.

As she struggled, the man told her that he wouldn't hurt her if she stopped struggling. She did, and he jammed a huge rag into her mouth to prevent her from screaming. Holding her arms behind her back, he pulled her skirt up and panties off. She kept struggling, but she was less than 1.5 meters tall and weighed only 43 kilos. Her attacker on the other hand was 2 meters and 115 kilos. She had no chance to prevent him from spreading her legs and raping her. She glanced down as he tried to enter her and realized that he was wearing a condom. At least she wouldn't get pregnant, but that didn't help her much. His attack was vicious but didn't last long.

As he finished and was still leaning over, her instinct for survival was strong enough that, even though she was lying down, she doubled her body up and kicked him twice, once in his face and once in his midsection. He uttered a curse and, throwing his whole weight

Chapter 1

behind his effort, he bodily picked her up and threw her against the stucco and stone wall of the nearest building. There was a sharp crack as her skull was shattered and her neck was broken.

He didn't even wonder how badly she was hurt. He was still too angry. He really didn't even care. He walked over to where she lay, quickly grabbed the rag from her mouth, and used it to wrap up the filled condom and his rubber gloves, making a nice ball of waste. As he warned himself that he'd better get away as soon as possible, he attended to himself, straightened his coat, and looked around to see if anyone was nearby or if anyone was coming to see what was happening. Seeing no one, he quickly walked down the alleyway in the direction that the woman had entered from the nearest street. Two blocks later he deposited his rag-wrapped package in a dumpster. After another couple of streets, he moved into another dark alleyway, removed his mask, and stuffed it into his coat pocket.

Why had he lost his temper? He really hadn't intended on hurting her. He only wanted to get rid of "the urge." He had hoped that maybe he would feel better if he could just have sex. Usually, in the past, he had courted women who willingly coupled with him, but he hadn't had anyone for several weeks. He hadn't felt that sense of belonging. And while he hadn't really cared for the women whom he dated, sex made him feel loved, accepted, and wanted - all the things he hadn't felt his entire lifetime.

"The urge" had become so strong in the last few days that when he had seen this girl, he knew he had to have her. He had followed her at a distance several evenings when she had left the library. He knew she walked these streets alone and would be easy to approach. He had noticed the streetlight flickering and going out the previous night and realized that the

The Urge

gods were smiling on him. Tonight, he had checked and, sure enough, the streetlight hadn't come on, so he waited for her to approach.

He'd waited in the darkest shadows until she had almost come upon him. It was fortuitous that she had been distracted by the light being off. He could get close to her without being seen. And, asking directions and pretending to be bitten by a dog, while being a last-minute idea, had worked very well. He laughed when he thought of the dog barking in the distance. Now he had to hurry home and take a hot shower. As he walked, he thought that if she were to be discovered, there wasn't a chance that he would ever be blamed for her being raped. He had taken every precaution. Good!

Unfortunately, lying in the alleyway behind him, with a fractured skull and broken neck, was a university student who had not only been raped but had been killed.

~ ~

Chapter 2
The Discovery

It was past midnight before the three roommates realized that Carmen hadn't come home from the library. Anna had already gone to bed. Paca, who also had a test the next day, had been studying in her room. Sylvia, who had cooked dinner, went into the kitchen for a drink of water and saw Carmen's uneaten dinner plate in the refrigerator.

Sylvia went to Carmen's room to see if she had come in unnoticed. The bed was made, and Carmen wasn't there. In fact, there was no indication that she'd ever come home - no book bag, no coat, no purse, nothing. Sylvia knocked on Paca's door and asked if she'd heard anything from Carmen. With a negative answer from Paca, Sylvia said that she also hadn't heard from her and that her untouched dinner was still in the kitchen. Looking at the clock, which now read one in the morning, they couldn't help but worry. After all, the university library closed at midnight; and, if Carmen had stayed until it closed, they were so close to the university that it took only fifteen minutes to

The Urge

walk to their apartment.

The two of them went to Anna's room and woke her. No, she also had heard nothing from Carmen. Anna suggested that maybe Carmen had run into a friend, and they had stopped at a local bar for a drink on the way home. They all agreed that might have happened until Paca reminded the other two that, with Carmen being the conscientious student that she was, she would never drink at a bar with a major test the next day. Carmen had been worrying about the exam all week. No, something might have happened. But what? They decided to wait, just in case she had stopped off for a drink, and then, if they hadn't heard anything, they would walk to the library themselves along the pathway which they knew Carmen usually walked in coming home. If they didn't find anything, they'd call the police. Something was wrong.

At two o'clock Carmen had still not come home. The three girls put on their coats, grabbed their cell phones, locked the door, and started walking toward the university. When they reached the dark alleyway, they remarked that the streetlight was out, and they needed to call the civil authorities to have it repaired. As they came abreast of the huge recycling bin, Anna stumbled over a large object in her path and almost fell. It was all she could do to remain upright as she grabbed at both her companions to keep on her feet.

Sylvia turned on her cell phone as a flashlight to see what Anna had stumbled over. Looking down, the three realized that the object was a bag of some variety. Looking closer, they recognized Carmen's book bag. What was it doing besides the recycling bin? Where was Carmen? Carmen wouldn't have left it here, of all places. Sylvia shouted, "Carmen, Carmen!" She waited a minute, then called again, "Carmen, Carmen!" There was no response in the dark alley.

Chapter 2

After standing together and discussing the bag for several minutes, they decided they needed to look around to see if Carmen had dropped anything else in the area. The alleyway was extremely dark, so they used the lights on their cell phones to fan out and check under and behind the bins. At first, nothing was found, but after about two minutes, Sylvia let out a scream as she discovered the still body of Carmen. The body was back further next to the building. Sylvia thought Carmen was just injured, but Carmen wasn't moving and was unresponsive to their voices.

The three girls decided not to touch anything else. They'd read enough detective stories to know that a crime scene had to be left alone for the police to get clues to solve the crime. While none of the three had any medical experience, Carmen looked very bad to them, even in the darkness. This had to be a crime scene.

Paca used her cell phone to call the police. She told them her name, the circumstances of looking for her missing roommate, her location, and what she and her two roommates had found. She was told not to touch anything, something they already knew, and that an officer would be arriving momentarily.

Indeed, it only took fifteen minutes for a police car and two officers to arrive at the site. Another five minutes and a second police car arrived with two more officers bearing huge floodlights. With their arrival, the three girls could see their former roommate lying next to the building. Carmen's neck was turned at an unusual angle, her head resembled a squashed casaba melon, her face had a deathly pallor, she was only partially clothed, and she wasn't breathing. Around her head was a halo of blood and other fluids that made her appear in the artificial light as though she were a saint or, God forbid, The Virgin Mary in a

The Urge

church painting.

Anna screamed, Paca fainted, and Sylvia started crying with huge sobs that shook her entire body. Anna cradled Paca and patted her until slowly Paca came to. All three girls were crying. Anna seemed to be the strongest of them. Somewhat recovering, she tried to calm her other two roommates. They had feared that something had happened to their friend, but the something that had happened was that Carmen was dead.

The first two police officers who had arrived pulled the girls to one side and got their statements. In their descriptions of what they had found when they had gotten there, they referred to Anna stumbling over Carmen's book bag. They went back to the recycling bin and showed it to the officers where it was still lying. The police officers took photographs of it in the place where it was found and marked the spot with evidence markers. They left it in place for later examination in case there were any clues to be found on it.

The second two police officers who had brought the lights called headquarters and requested that their head investigator, Detective Mendoza, and the coroner come immediately to the crime scene.

As the girls continued giving their statement to the first two police officers, they shared that their now-dead roommate hadn't really been missed until almost one o'clock. While she should have been home around twelve-fifteen if she had stayed until the library closed at midnight, they had waited to search for her until two o'clock, in the hopes that she had met someone and had stopped at a local bar. As Paca, sobbing, said that maybe if they'd searched for her sooner Carmen might have still been alive, Lieutenant Mendoza and the coroner arrived. Both looked like they had just

Chapter 2

been roused from bed and thrown on their clothes.

The coroner, besides being unshaven, was rumpled and bleary-eyed. Taking a quick look at the victim, he became fully awake and started a thorough examination of the entire area. He decided with the trash trucks arriving within the hour, he had a very limited time frame to discover any clues to this horrible murder.

Detective Mendoza and the coroner tried to catalog everything within the crime scene while the girls continued their story of the night. The detective and coroner asked about where the book bag had been found and were shown the marker and the bag. They photographed, tagged, and collected it. They measured the distance between that spot and where they saw scuff marks and ruts in the dust and debris where the victim had been dragged. It looked like a scuffle had occurred. They measured the distance between where these marks ended and where the body was lying - a full two meters away. There were no other marks between these last two spots.

How had the body come to be where it was? Could the body have been carried there? Or had the body been thrown there? If so, by one or two people? If it were two men, it might be easily done; but, if by one person, the attacker would have had to have been very large or very strong.

The coroner assumed the attacker or attackers were a man or men from the lack of clothes on the victim's lower body. It appeared she had been raped. While it was a guess, he'd seen too many rape victims in his life not to recognize all the signs. He'd know more when he could complete an autopsy and determine if there had been penetration. Hopefully, the presence of semen or other material, if he were lucky, would

The Urge

give him a DNA sample of the rapist or rapists.

Looking at the victim's head and the angle of her neck, he could see that her neck was broken, and her skull was crushed. The cerebral spinal fluid and blood around her head had formed a significant puddle and the blood was now starting to coagulate. That would place the murder around midnight. If she had been thrown by one man to accomplish this, he would have had to have been very large or very strong. He proceeded to take photographs of the scene until he thought he had enough information to proceed further with lab analyses. He and one of the police officers put the victim's body in a body bag so that he could transport it back to the morgue. He also retrieved the victim's book bag from the detective to take that with him as well.

Detective Mendoza finished speaking with the girls and the two police officers who had been interviewing them. The girls continued to berate themselves that maybe Carmen would have been alive if they had searched for her sooner. Lieutenant Mendoza assured them that from his quick observation of the crime scene, Carmen had probably died instantaneously when her head had hit the wall. At least that made Paca feel somewhat better, but not really -- her friend was gone.

The police officers told the girls to return to their apartment and stay there. He asked them to give him the name, address, and phone number of Carmen's parents. Since they didn't have that information with them, they said that they would email him that information and asked for the officer's email address. He also gave them his phone number at the station in case they remembered anything else he should know. He stated that he would contact Carmen's parents with the sad news as soon as he received the contact

Chapter 2

information from the girls. He thanked them for their cooperation and murmured some words of comfort over the loss of their friend. He knew it wasn't going to help, but maybe time would make them heal.

As the coroner and detective reviewed the area before leaving, they exchanged looks and shook their heads. The coroner thought to himself that this was such a sad scene. What a tragedy! What a senseless crime! Another young woman whose life had needlessly been ended. He hoped this would be the last time he'd see a scene like this. He prayed this would be a singular incidence. He hoped this rape and killing was a one-time crime. But it looked too clean. It looked as though, not only did the attacker know what he was doing, but he'd been very careful to clean up after himself. If he was as careful as the coroner thought, there would be no semen and no DNA sample to tie anyone to the rape. But murder too, that was unusual; rapists usually didn't kill their victims.

~ ~

Chapter 3
New Victims

Several weeks later "the urge" again was being experienced. Even though the attacker had read in the newspapers that he had killed the victim the night he raped her, he realized that he'd gotten away with it. The police had no idea about his identity. There were no witnesses. No one had even heard anything during the attack. No one came forward with any ideas about who the attacker might be. He'd gotten very lucky. He still had made no lady friends that he could "get close to." It was as if the world had turned its back on him. Déjà vu.

One evening as he walked the Madrid streets in the old town after midnight, he passed by a supermarket that boasted of being open 24 hours every day, except Sunday. He stood in a darkened doorway across the street, which was at an angle where he could see the supermarket front door, but anyone standing there couldn't see him. He realized that this might be a perfect location to find a woman to take care of his "urge." He went home and decided to return to that

The Urge

location the next night, but the next night he would be prepared in case he got lucky.

The next day he was so hopped up that he could hardly function at work. Fortunately, no one noticed his agitation, and as evening approached, he made sure to have a condom, rubber gloves, a cloth rag, and his mask in his pocket as he left home. He walked the distance to his lookout post and decided to wait, no matter how long that might be until he could satisfy the "urge." He put on his rubber gloves and mask. As the nearest church bell chimed two in the morning, a smaller-than-average-sized, middle-aged woman left the store carrying two large bags and a smaller one. She walked away from the store. He felt the erection working as he waited until she had turned the corner. He reached into his pocket checking to see that he did have the condom. He walked after her. She wasn't exactly "his type", but her size was, and that fact was a bonus. Also, she was distracted, trying to carry her bags. She walked slowly enough that he quickly caught up with her as she turned down a darker side street. As he walked past her, he bumped into her, as if by accident. She had dropped the smaller package and was attempting to pick it up from the sidewalk while maintaining her grip on the two larger bags. With a gentlemanly voice, he apologized to her and offered to help her. She was so upset with having dropped the bag that she scarcely looked at him but did accept his help. He picked up her smaller bag, approached her, and, as she stopped, he dropped the bag again. He grabbed her with one hand and used the other hand to stuff the rag into her mouth to prevent her from screaming. As she attempted to push him away, the other two larger bags fell to the ground. Both he and the woman ignored them as they scuffled.

He pulled her into a darker area of the street,

Chapter 3

pushed her down, and told her softly to stop struggling. He said he wasn't going to hurt her. At that point, he opened her coat, pulled down her slacks and panties, slid the condom over his member, and raped her. She had worked all day and half the night and was too physically tired to do anything other than comply.

When he was finished, he doubled up his fist and hit her in the jaw. She lost consciousness and lay silently. He took the rag out from her mouth, took off the condom, wrapped it and his rubber gloves in the rag. Looking around and seeing a trash bin about three blocks down the street, he walked there and took his trash to the bin and deposited it. Several blocks further down the street he removed his mask and put it in his pocket. Oh - he felt so much better.

As he walked home, he remembered the first time he'd forced himself on a girl. His parents had been involved in a huge argument about him with both his parents yelling that he could never do anything right and what a mistake he had been. They should have never had "this child." While his father had tried to defend him somewhat because he was starting to succeed in school, his mother remarked that his recent success still didn't matter. She didn't want him around. She was sick of seeing his face. He was getting so tall and eating them out of house and home. Besides using all their money to feed him, his soft voice was almost effeminate. Was he some sort of a weirdo? What did all their friends think about them having such a strange child?

He'd run out of the apartment and kept running until he had no energy left. He really hadn't known where he was going. It was much later, and he had ended up several kilometers from his village, and in the next village near its school. He went into the playground and sat on one of the swings. As he rocked

The Urge

back and forth, he saw some other teenagers over on the next block. There were at least five of them. They seemed to be arguing, just like his parents had argued, and he wondered why the whole world seemed to be at odds with itself. As he watched, four of them walked away from the fifth, a smaller girl, who seemed to be crying.

She walked in the opposite direction from the others, she came in his direction. He didn't move. As he watched her, he started to have a strange feeling. At the time he didn't realize what it was. He'd never had sex before. He felt his penis start to engorge as he watched the girl coming toward him. He also felt an excitement that was strangely wonderful. As she walked into the playground, she suddenly realized that she wasn't alone. He got up from the swing and approached her, gently asking why she was crying and if he could do anything to help her. She sobbed even louder. Since she wasn't really looking at him, he didn't feel subconscious as he walked over to her. He took her into his arms and started stroking her back. She clung to him as he half-carried her and half-walked her over to a darkened corner of the playground. Before she could object, he had pushed her jeans and panties down and had entered her.

Boy, had he been dumb. He hadn't even had on a condom at that time, but he'd gotten by with it. He didn't think that she had even looked at him so she would have no description of him to tell her parents or anyone else. He had hit her and knocked her out before she could scream. He left the area quickly and went home. The memory came to him as if it had been yesterday. And he knew that over the years the same memory came back often enough to know that he knew how to solve his problems whenever they resurfaced.

Now, he knew what the feeling had been in that

Chapter 3

time long past. It had been "the urge" - but in a lesser-felt-way than the way he experienced it as he aged. With his increasing years, "the urge" had increased in intensity. It became a strong feeling of need and acceptance that never seemed to be satisfied. In the moment of sexual arousal and climax, he felt accepted. And every time, he had rejected his victim, it was before she realized what had happened and could reject him. HE had rejected HER. HE was in control, not someone else. HE didn't need his parents' or anyone else's acceptance. HE could find acceptance anywhere. HE was in control of his life. What he could barely control was "the urge." It became the overpowering director of his life, never really satisfied and returning again and again.

Reaching home, he showered and went to bed, just as he was doing now. A good hot shower would feel wonderful. Without a thought about the middle-aged woman lying unconscious in the street behind him, he continued home. After all, he needed his rest to function at work tomorrow.

He did function very well the next day - and the next - until about three weeks later when he again started getting "the urge."

He had been returning from a visit to an art gallery opening where a friend of his had just been admitted and was having his works shown there for the first time. He'd gone as an invited guest and had experienced a lovely evening. As the fiesta had come to a close, and gallery owner stated that everyone should return during the exhibit to again study the lovely artworks.

Several of the other guests nodded their heads and agreed that would be very nice. He decided that maybe he might return again too. The wine had flowed in abundance all night and the patrons seemed to not

The Urge

be thinking nor feeling much of anything except the wine. He might get lucky.

The next night he did return, but he stayed outside in the shadows, armed with the mask, a rag, rubber gloves, and a condom.

And he was lucky. One of the silly little young women broke off from her companions after walking for several blocks. She was very petite and had obviously had way too much wine. She was staggering slightly as he caught up to her just before she entered a park located five blocks from the gallery. He bumped into her, sending her sprawling into a dark bush. As she fell, she took a look at his face and realized he looked somewhat familiar, but she couldn't put a name to the face. Maybe she had drunk more than she had thought. Everything was really fuzzy. But before she could say anything, he stuffed the rag into her mouth and attacked her. She was groped and then raped. He was happy because she neither fought him nor did she resist in any way. She was so limp that he could easily enter her and dispense with "the urge." After he was finished, even though she seemed to be completely oblivious to anything happening to her, he knocked her out with his fist, removed the filled condom, wrapped it in the rag with the rubber gloves. He made a deposit in a garbage bin several blocks away and placed his mask in his jacket pocket.

Both the middle-aged shopper and the young woman reported to the police that they had been raped, but there were no witnesses and there were no suspects. They were examined, but neither had any semen or other evidence in or on them. There was no chance for the police to obtain a DNA sample from either. The middle-aged woman could give no description of her assailant, but the young woman said that the man "looked sort of familiar." Both described their attacker

Chapter 3

as tall, slender, but very muscular and strong. Both described him as being soft-spoken and polite.

The police were baffled. It was becoming obvious to them they had a serial rapist working in the Madrid area, but they had no clue as to his identity, nor location, as all three rapes had occurred in different areas of Madrid. What they did know was that the M.O. in these last two known cases was identical - the man had bumped into his victims to stop them, had gagged them, had raped them, and had hit them, knocking them out, so that he could escape.

~ ~

Chapter 4
Diego and Marielena

Police Commissioner Diego Rivera Hernandez Pizzaro Bolivar sat at his desk. On this day, the police station was peaceful and quiet, so he had some time to consider his life both past and present. During the last year-and-a-half, his life had changed dramatically. He had changed from being a lonely widower, bereaved at the death of his beloved wife, Amaya, to a happily married man with a new wife, Marielena. Previously he had thought life held no promise for him. Amaya's death from colon cancer had left him devastated. He had become engrossed in the brutal murder of Margarita Elliot, who had been Miss Spain and Miss World and had become the wife of Lord Charles Elliot, a wealthy Englishman. The Elliots had purchased the largest villa in San Anton and had been living there for four years when the murder occurred. Diego remembered the morning when he had been called to the villa by its staff and discovered the wife's bloody body with the antique dagger lying next to it on the floor of the second-floor temporary art studio. Being held by the

The Urge

housekeeper and the gardener was a very scared young artist who had been hired to paint Margarita's portrait. This artist later became his friend; then his girlfriend; still later his fiancée; and now she was his new wife.

It had taken Diego quite a while to change his initial impression of Marielena. During that time, he had developed a healthy respect for her ability as an artist and helped her get her painting into the Prado. He had also developed a professional respect for her ability to put facts together to reach conclusions as a detective. After the murder had been solved, he had offered her a part-time job as a detective in his department.

But even more fabulous and wonderful, he had fallen in love with her. She was an exceptional woman who had fallen on hard times but had risen above all her circumstances. Through time, he had decided that she could be a perfect potential second wife to him, and he had proposed. He had been delighted that she had also fallen in love with him and joyfully accepted his proposal. Now, being happily married, they formed a powerful partnership in the police department and a powerful partnership at home. They had become inseparable.

Since Marielena had not been properly trained in law enforcement prior to his offer of the part-time detective position, his first step was to send her to the Madrid police academy to be trained. While she was slightly built and barely a meter-and-a-half tall, she was wiry and strong. She quickly became a very good police officer. Where she excelled most was in the area of, almost instinctively, knowing what was happening around her - the same characteristic which she had displayed during the Margarita murder investigation. Since being a police officer was only part-time, she had time to continue her original profession of being

Chapter 4

an artist. Indeed, today she was back out in their village sketching in preparation for painting her many canvases depicting Spanish life and people. Many of these paintings were finding their way into homes, businesses, and museums all over the world. After it became known that her painting "The Spanish Beauty" had been purchased by the Prado, she experienced a robust growth in commissions and sales. His wife was a fabulously talented artist who was now having many well-deserved successes. He was so proud of her.

They had sold his cramped apartment in which he had lived with his first wife, Amaya, and had purchased a small house near the house of Señora Santiago, where Marielena had lived when they met. The Señora was delighted to have them as neighbors. She had loved Marielena when she had lived in her home and was happy that he and Marielena had married. Amaya's parents, as well as his own parents, had died last year. Señora Santiago had been adopted by both he and Marielena, almost as another parent; and, whenever he was looking for Marielena, he could usually find her socializing over at Señor Santiago's house. Marielena's parents who lived near Rhonda came periodically and embraced Señora Santiago as well. It was as if they were all part of an extended family.

Diego and Marielena had found each other at a propitious time in both their lives. Both had been extremely lonely, had much in common, and had found characteristics in each other to compliment themselves. It had been a short, but wonderful courtship with the inhabitants of the entire village as spectators and cheerleaders for these two fantastic people. Even though he had initially thought that she was too young for him to court much less marry, her intellect, boundless energy, and talents had enabled him to become younger. He now acted and felt closer

The Urge

to her age than his actual age. They were a great match and loved each other very much.

As the summer light dimmed and the dinner hour approached, Marielena came into the office with her rucksack of art supplies flung over her back. They had arranged to meet there and walk back to their house together after a day's work. Perhaps they'd stop at the Belloto for tapas and a caña before going home to a quick dinner and bed. After all, their first date had been at the Belloto, and it was as if the owners felt part of their family as well. He was a happy man and she a happy woman. They shared a good life.

~ ~

Chapter 5
Continuing Rapes

The rapist couldn't stand it. It seemed to him that "the urge", while satisfied temporarily with each rape, intensified the next episode of desire to even greater heights. How could this be? He had been able to control "the urge" for many years, taking only one or two victims per year. Between rapes, he had always dated. He knew women found him attractive and would willingly couple with him when he made known to them that he found them desirable. Most of the rapes had been in Spain, but some of his rapes had occurred in other countries when he was on a business trip or a vacation. He'd been very fortunate that they hadn't been recognized as being linked or that the police hadn't focused on one perpetrator doing them all.

But now, "the urge" he was experiencing was growing in strength and becoming more frequent. What was he to do? At times, he seemed unable to even concentrate on his work. One rape seemed to be leading to another and then still another. He lived his waking hours either at work or out roaming the

The Urge

streets looking for new victims. He enlarged his search area. Beside Madrid, he included Toledo, Salamanca, Segovia, and Guadalajara. He was smart enough to realize that, if he concentrated all his rapes in one geographic area, it would be more likely to have them linked and to have the police realize they were dealing with one man, not several. The result would be his arrest and incarceration. That could not happen.

Maybe, he reasoned, it was time to find a job in a new location. But to move meant that he would have to leave Madrid and all the things he loved to do, see, and experience. It would mean leaving a job that he absolutely loved. A job which he had prepared himself his entire lifetime. A job in which he could immerse himself. A job that might not be found in a comparably exciting location. If he went elsewhere, he might have to settle for something totally not to his liking and experience. No, he'd just have to be more careful. It was not a matter of stopping what he was doing. "The urge" was too strong. He was between a rock and a hard place.

That night he took the train up to Salamanca to spend the weekend. He took a small room in a nondescript hotel and went hunting. Strangers in Salamanca were common. As a university town and a tourist location, people were always visiting there - parents of students, tourists from all over the world, and people who had business with the professors at the university or the university itself. But, just in case, he had come prepared. Just in case, he got lucky this weekend.

He left his room and wandered the streets. He looked for possible attack sites, as well as possible victims. He was amazed by the variety in choices for both. Lots of beautiful, small, young women. Lots of bars where those young women would become

Chapter 5

inebriated. Lots of dark alleys to choose from. It was a rapist's cornucopia of possible delights. And, with these same young women feeling perfectly at home in their university town, their stomping grounds, they were oblivious to the possible dangers that they might face. They had become blind. Just the right kind of victim - careless, carefree, and stupid.

He was looking at Salamanca as a child would look through the windows of a candy store. The young students here were as unsuspecting as the university student whom he had accidentally murdered in Madrid. He was delighted to have come prepared this weekend. He would definitely find himself lucky sometime during this trip. All he had to do was just be careful.

At last, he found the appropriate spot. He had wandered into a tapas bar near the old town of the city and discovered that it was being frequented by university students. It had an especially dark alleyway behind it. He knew this was where he would go hunting late Saturday evening. Today was only Friday so he could relax and enjoy his surroundings.

With one location found, he'd do the bar scene and scope out other locations. It might be that he could find an even better spot or find another area that could be used for a different victim some later time. After several hours he stopped at a restaurant for dinner. He found a second bar and had several drinks before going back to his hotel with a full stomach, a relaxed body, and a happy feeling that "the urge" was soon to be satisfied.

During the day on Saturday, he people-watched and went to various churches and tourist sites. One of the churches had possibilities for a hunt some other time. It was too bad he'd planned to be here in Salamanca

The Urge

only this weekend, but there were other weeks and weekends. He really wasn't worried since any attacks here couldn't be linked to a rapist in Madrid. It was amazing to him that when he knew that "the urge" was going to be satisfied, he could be so calm and calculating.

Early Saturday evening he prepared. His excitement was starting to build. "The urge" almost overcame him. He could feel it becoming stronger with anticipation. He knew he would satisfy it and return to Madrid being relaxed. He filled his pockets with the necessary items.

He had a drink at the hotel bar before he left for a late dinner at a small restaurant he hadn't been to before. He knew, if he appeared at the same places multiple times, bartenders and waiters or waitresses were very astute in noticing their customers. It was part of how they made most of their income, knowing and catering to repeat customers. If one were recognized as becoming a repeat- customer, he would increase his chances of being caught. That would never do. He had to remain inconspicuous.

After his dinner, he walked the streets and watched. As the hour became later, he prowled like a hungry lion. He remembered a wildlife video on TV that talked about lions and other predators cutting out their prey from an active and protective herd. His possible prey was becoming more inebriated and less cautious. As he finally retreated to his chosen spot, he realized that now he would have to make a choice.

Finally, he saw her. His heart jumped in his chest. She was perfect. Petite and drunk. She had waved farewell to her companions and was weaving in his direction. She stopped once by a wall to steady herself. As she started walking again, she stumbled. Again, she steadied herself on the nearest wall.

Chapter 5

He put on his rubber gloves and positioned his mask. Then, as she stumbled past him, he bumped into her. Apologizing profusely, he offered her his hand. She looked up at him and held out her hand to him. That was all he needed. He took the rag and gagged her, pulling her into the shadows.

They were the only ones in this side street behind the bar, and, while she was too drunk to put up much of a fight, "the urge" provided him with the excess adrenalin rush to overcome her. He quickly put on the condom and pushed up her short, little skirt university students preferred. Her panties were little abbreviated thongs which he quickly tore aside. So easy! Why didn't women drink more responsibly? Why did young women drink to excess such that they were unaware of their surroundings? Why did young women leave their friends and walk alone and unprotected in areas which would usually be safe in the daylight, but become the hunting grounds of men like him at night? Why didn't these women call for and take a taxi home when they were alone, especially alone and drunk? Didn't these women have parents who warned them of what might happen to them? Or were they choosing to ignore any warnings and thought "it can't happen to me"? He remembered the years when he'd been in college listening to other male students talk about their exploits with females. They'd laughed and applauded each other bragging about their "date rapes" and how all they noticed about their fellow female students was how sexy they looked and all they were "good for" was a sexual release. Most of his fellow students were wrong in blaming the rapes on the girls. These guys knew what they wanted. The girls were dumb. Date rape was common then and also now, he read the newspapers. Didn't women realize they needed to be careful of ALL men? He didn't know the answers to these questions, but all these coincidences - women being

The Urge

unaware of their surroundings, being unprotected, being drunk, or being alone on dark streets - made life for him a wonderful playground of enjoyment. As he remembered those college days, feelings of his own inadequacies reared their ugly heads again. It was in college that he realized how different he was from his male classmates. They looked at women as sex objects. He looked at women, especially small or petite ones as a release for his "urge". He didn't care about the age, occupation, or clothing of the victim. It didn't matter at all. In fact, he was like the rapist in an interview that he'd read about in a newspaper who had raped a nun in her habit. Women to him were only a temporary release from "the urge". He needed women only as his one-at-a-time fulfillment of feeling wanted and needed. He had had a professor once that looked at his art, both subject matter and execution, and suggested that he might have need of some counseling, but he had refused.

As his mind came back to the present and he continued to rape this latest victim, she seemed to become more awake; but, as he finished, she slumped over becoming unconscious. Definitely, too much to drink. He laughed to himself. She was so out of it that he didn't even need to hit her into unconsciousness to make his escape. He wrapped the condom in the rag with his rubber gloves, rearranged his clothing, and strode off. His victim lay where he had raped her. A couple of blocks away he dumped his rape remains in a dumpster; further on he removed his mask and put it in his pocket.

The night had been such an easy evening that he decided to stop and have a glass of wine to celebrate before returning to his hotel. While at the bar, a young woman attempted to pick him up. Wow! This was his lucky night! After sharing a bottle and a half of wine with

Chapter 5

the woman drinking most of it, he accompanied her to her hotel room. He laughed when he realized that he didn't have an extra condom. She opened the bedtable and gave him one of a supply she had. Obviously, she had planned for the evening's entertainment. They seemed very compatible with each other and quickly coupled. Afterward, she, slurring her words, wanted him to stay the rest of the night. When he said, "No", she hit him. He pushed her back and her head struck the headboard knocking her out. He quickly retreated and went to his own hotel. How lucky could he be - a two-rape night!

Later in his own room, he mused. Why would a woman try to pick up a strange man for a date in a bar? Didn't women have any idea about the possibility that in their drunken state, they might choose to meet up, flirt, and go somewhere else with the wrong person? Someone like him? Such women made life interesting for men who wanted only one thing: sex.

Two weeks later when he was again visiting Salamanca, he accepted another invitation from a woman in a bar. Although it was a different bar and a different woman, this woman was again inebriated and slid into a seat near him at the bar hoping to get some free drinks and conversation. She made all the advances toward him to his and the bartender's amusement. After a few more drinks she invited him to take her home. He did. And one thing led to another. He really didn't consider it rape, although technically it was. He doubted that she would consider it rape. He hadn't picked her up or attacked her. She had picked him up. The result was that "the urge" was fulfilled without any threat to his being discovered and arrested.

~ ~

Chapter 6
Marielena's Assignment

While San Anton and Toledo remained unscathed by reports of rape, the police station was well aware of the rape reports in Madrid and other areas of Spain. In the past handful of months, there had been several more reports of rapes. In one report from Salamanca, a student was raped behind a bar frequented by university students. There was another report from Madrid where a young businesswoman had worked late and was on her way home when she had been raped. From Guadalajara came a report where a young female tourist had been raped in an alley behind the train station. And, from another part of Madrid came the unacceptable report that a young woman, who had left Confession late on a Saturday evening, had been attacked and raped behind the church.

Commissioner Rivera and his wife and part-time detective, Marielena Cortez, read each report and remarked that it was only a matter of time before the women in Toledo and San Anton might be targeted. It seemed that the rapist, a serial rapist they decided,

The Urge

was coming closer to them and their locale. It seemed the rapist was moving his location but continued to work in Madrid and its surrounding cities.

Commissioner Rivera, knowing that Marielena was good at figuring out puzzles, decided to put her in charge of compiling a list of the rape victims, the characteristics of the women who were being victimized, and the locations of their attacks. Maybe the rapist was looking for a particular type of woman as a victim.

Marielena suggested that perhaps she should search the literature on rapists to come up with a list of traits that characterized serial rapists. Marielena already knew a few things about rapists - her own sister had been a rape victim. She set to work by Googling the term "serial rapist." She discovered a profile of the types of personal and personality traits most common to serial rapists according to scientific research. She was amazed. Taking out a notebook, she wrote down the following:

Psychological evidence indicating the rapist had been rejected, especially when young. The sexual act of rape made the rapist feel accepted/loved.

Most had never been recognized as having problems at all in their past.

A number of them were left-handed.

They usually had access to young females or went out of their way to have access to young females.

There were conflicting reports on what was "the trigger" for their crime or about the frequency of their crime.

Very seldom did they hurt their victim physically, other than the rape, which while physical, was more

Chapter 6

devastating psychologically to the victim.

Only rarely was the victim killed.

Marielena researched the cases of rape within the Madrid area over the last three years. As a detective and member of a police force, she was able to access all the files from various police districts. She made three lists: the victims' names with physical characteristics; locations where the rapes had occurred; and the types of areas in these locations which the rapist had chosen for his attack points. One thing jumped out to her immediately. All the women, regardless of age, had been under 1-and-a-half meters in height and approximately 40 kilos. The locations varied and the areas varied, but this rapist knew precisely what kind of woman he was looking for. He was extremely consistent in his choice of victim.

When she took her list to show her husband, the Commissioner, he sat for a moment thinking. Then, looking up at her, he said, "You do realize that those body dimensions of the victims match your personal dimensions exactly?"

Marielena gasped and said, "Oh - they do. That thought completely escaped me. But what didn't escape me is that we don't have the complete police files. We don't have any of the descriptions or the details that the victims told the police in their interviews after the rapes. In order for me to do anything specific with these lists, I need more information from the victims themselves."

"What bothers me is that you fit the description of the victims," said Commissioner Rivera very softly. "I know you've had training at the police academy, but I'm not sure that's enough. I want you to start taking a martial arts class in self-defense. I'd never forgive myself if you were attacked and didn't have all the

The Urge

training you needed to defend yourself. And we both agree that it is only a matter of time before the rapist moves into our area."

After a moment of hesitation, Marielena said, "I appreciate that - and - maybe you're right. OK, I'll enroll in a class tomorrow."

"You can take the training and still get paid on your workdays. It can be considered additional police training. I'll see if we can arrange for private lessons during the day and, perhaps, a crash course during the next few weeks. I'd feel a lot safer if you had some training in self-defense, both when you're on duty but also when you're out doing your sketching and painting."

"I'll call tomorrow to see about it."

"No, I'll call today," he said.

"In the meantime, what do I do about the victims' statements to the police about their rapes?"

"Let me contact the Madrid police department. I'm still in touch with a few of my former colleagues from working there. Maybe I can get you the information or maybe I can arrange for you to speak directly to the victims yourself. They may have remembered more about the rape since their initial police interviews."

Marielena went to her desk to finish working on her information list. While there, she received a letter in the mail. Looking at the envelope she was confused. Why would the city council members send a letter to her and not the Police Commissioner? After all, she was only a part-time detective.

As she opened the envelope and started reading, her eyes opened wide with surprise. The letter had nothing to do with police work or her job as a part-

Chapter 6

time detective. No wonder it wasn't addressed to the police commissioner. This letter concerned her other occupation - being an artist.

As she read the contents, she was filled with the immense significance of its content. While she didn't always consider her artwork made her famous, the people in the village of San Anton knew it had been accepted into the Prado in Madrid and recognized her talents. They were used to seeing her in the streets painting and sketching. She had become known as "our local town artist." It was also known that she was married to the local town boy who had "made good" by becoming their police commissioner. This letter confirmed it. The town council had passed a resolution that she should be hired to paint a mural in the town hall. She was to have another commission.

Wow! She'd never painted a mural before. That would be a new experience. But - she painted in acrylics, which were really no different than house paint in many respects. She had whitewashed the outer walls of her family's home in Rhonda and helped paint interior walls too. So how much different would it be from painting landscapes and seascapes on canvases - perhaps the same, only bigger. Of course, she had to accept this commission. What an honor! But what did they want to portray in the mural?

She probably needed to have a talk with the council members further about the purpose they had in mind for the mural. She would have to compile a list of things they wanted in the mural, make sketches, prepare the wall in question, get supplies, and have preliminary ideas accepted by the council before she could ever begin painting. And what would she be paid for her efforts?

She had just thought the preceding day about how

routine her life had become. Now she had three major jobs to accomplish: take a martial arts class, compile information for a police investigation, and paint a mural. Her life had just become very complicated in a matter of one day.

She rushed into her husband's office to share her good fortune. He was as happy as she was to hear about her painting the town hall mural. He reminded her that he had foreseen she would be in demand due to her art being purchased by the Prado. He shared his news with her. He had, true to his word, called the Chow Tu Martial Arts Studio in downtown Toledo and arranged for a compressed series of lessons in self-defense. They would start the next day. The Studio had clothes that she could purchase and in which she could take her classes. Master Chow Un Mi would himself teach her and promised that within only a matter of four weeks, she would be proficient enough to defend herself. The two men had agreed that Diego's suggestion to take the class was a good idea and that Marielena's self-protection was all that mattered.

As evening approached, they closed their offices, leaving Deputy Ortega in charge of the station, and went home.

~ ~

Chapter 7
Marielena Tackles Three Jobs

The following morning before Marielena went into Toledo for her first martial arts lesson, she went to the town hall to speak with the mayor and one of the town hall council members concerning the art commission of painting the town hall mural. She expressed to them how appreciative she was of the honor to paint a mural in her adopted home village. They assured her of their happiness to have her living in their village and how pleased and proud they were of her nationally recognized success. When they quoted the amount of money that they were willing to pay for her work, she was surprised. She knew the village was one of the wealthier suburbs of Toledo, but the amount was not insignificant. It was a real vote of confidence in her abilities. When she asked about the subject matter to be in the mural, she was pleased to learn that the artwork wanted was "right up her alley". They wanted to show the landscapes surrounding the village, the village itself as seen from a distance, and village scenes, such as the main square, the Catholic

The Urge

church, and properties owned by local citizens. As far as background material for the mural, all she had done over the time she had lived there was appropriate. A piece of cake! She left the mayor's office with a song in her heart and a smile on her face.

Her next stop that morning was the Chow Tu Martial Arts Studio. Here the results were much more disturbing. She spent more time lying on the canvas which covered the floor than standing. The proprietor, Master Chow Un Mi was reassuring in his words, reminding her that what she was trying to do was compress several years' worth of lessons into a few weeks. He encouraged her to practice all the movements at home between lessons. She went home both physically and mentally bruised. Nonetheless, she was determined and worked on the movements for several hours before grabbing a quick lunch and going to the police station to work the late afternoon-early evening shift.

While she had been at the town hall and at the martial arts lesson, Diego had talked to his colleagues at the main Madrid police station. It had been a very productive discussion. They had come up with the same conclusions about where the rapist was located and how he proceeded to attack his victims but were no further along in finding him. They had not yet reached Marielena's conclusion about the physical characteristics of the victims. Their police artist had died several months ago, and they hadn't filled his vacant job. They, therefore, hadn't gotten any clear image from their victims concerning either what the rapist might look like or what his potential victims could look like, either.

When Diego mentioned that his wife, also one of his detectives, was working on the case and was also an artist, his Madrid friend, Detective José Martinez

Chapter 7

Ruiz Castillo Iglesia, suggested that not only should Marielena come to Madrid and talk with all the victims to compile their stories, but that she should talk to them about what the rapist looked like and, perhaps, make a sketch of the man. Diego and José agreed that maybe speaking to a woman would be easier for the victims. If Marielena bonded with the women, their relationship could make them speak more readily about any impressions they had of the rapist. They knew a relaxed witness sometimes was able to remember more than they had during their first interview after their rapes. José said that all the victims he'd had contact with appeared to be in shock and unable to cope with, not only the attacks but also, their own feelings of guilt at not recognizing that they had been in danger. Now the problem was how could they arrange Marielena's schedule to do all the jobs which she now had. Priorities?

Tuesday morning while Marielena was taking her first martial arts class, a new rape report came in from Seville. It had happened during the past Saturday night but was only now being reported by the police because of the time spent analyzing any DNA from the victim. The M.O. was the same - a slight-built young woman named Marisol Huavos Juarez Rios Ramerez, late at night after drinking and arguing with her boyfriend had wandered along the riverfront and had been attacked in a shady area where the streetlights hadn't been very bright. Besides being raped, she had suffered cuts and bruises because she had fought her attacker. She, unlike some of the other victims, had managed to scratch her attacker's arm. And she, unlike any of the other victims, had the attacker's skin cells underneath her fingernails. Again, she had been hit and knocked out after the rape so that the rapist could escape. But this time, he had left behind some important DNA, which they could link to him.

The Urge

Unfortunately, when the sample was run through the Spanish DNA criminal files, there were no matches. They were no further in finding the rapist than they had been before. At least, whenever they did find him, they would have proof that he had committed this one rape.

When Marielena returned to the station, she added all the data from this report to her list of facts and victims. She would have to go to Seville to see this victim and talk to her since several bits of information were missing or didn't make sense. What was a description of this victim? What did the rapist look like? She also noted the longer distance between Madrid and Seville. Did this indicate that perhaps the rapist was widening his hunting territory? If so, what would be the effect on their search for him?

During the next three weeks, Marielena spent her mornings at the Chow Tu Martial Arts Studio. She was slowly improving and spent more time on her feet than on the mats. She was determined to learn, and Master Chow Un Mi complimented her, but she still had much to learn. Her wiriness and body strength helped her, as did her intelligence. She now knew what to do, but it was a matter of practice. Her afternoons were spent either at the police station or at home, reviewing her many sketches of the village in an attempt to choose which ones to include in the city hall mural.

One afternoon she took a portfolio to the mayor's office with a concept drawing of her individual sketches and how they could be incorporated to compose a cohesive mural. While most of her ideas were quickly approved, several sketches of individual businesses and the village Catholic church appeared to be done at a different angle than the mayor and the council members wished. He did approve of the overall mural design and was pleased by her presentation.

Chapter 7

The next day, after her martial arts lesson, she returned to the village streets with her sketchbook. Now that she realized what was required, she could make some new sketches from the desired vantage points. She also started to make a list of painting supplies. It would take several weeks of full-time painting to complete the actual mural. The wall was quite large - at least 12 meters by 15 meters, but with her working on it only part-time during afternoons, she anticipated at least two months, maybe three, would be required to paint and seal the entire mural. She could hardly wait to start the actual painting.

It was a good thing that her hours at the martial arts lessons were being considered part of her detective work hours. It meant her mornings were being paid. That, plus some afternoon hours had given her an income; but so far, she hadn't been able to sketch and paint in the village as she had done previously. She found herself even working in the evenings at home refining her sketches for the mural. It reminded her of her busy days at the Elliot villa when she worked on her friend's portrait.

One afternoon when she had stopped briefly at Señora Santiago's house on the way home, she apologized to her for not seeing her very often in the past few weeks.

Señora Santiago said, "My dear, you look tired."

Marielena said, "I am, but I'm happy. I feel that I'm accomplishing something with my life. It's so different having a husband beside me to share everything in life. Diego is so good to me. I came to share some news - the town council has hired me to do a mural in the city hall. And Diego set up for me to take martial arts self-defense lessons."

Señora Santiago said, "Good, you're such a little

The Urge

thing. I've wondered about whether you'd be able to fend off a criminal in an emergency. But now, I won't be as worried. You and Diego were meant to be together. I'm glad he is watching out for you. You're both very good people. You do need to try to get more rest, or you'll not be able to enjoy each other. It may be difficult to not overextend yourself, you're so conscientious; but you need to find a balance between your work and your personal life, so you don't get burned out."

Marielena thought as she left and went home, Señora Satiago's words were filled with wisdom. She was glad she'd shared with her the news about the mural and about taking self-defense lessons. The thought of the jobs had made both her friend and her happy. The mural would mean more income and make her feel more confident in her abilities as an artist. And the lessons were making her feel more confident in her abilities as a policewoman.

~ ~

Chapter 8
More Information

The next six weeks were busy ones. Marielena finished her lessons with Master Chow, who cautioned her to keep practicing and not to be over-confidant. She purchased the paints and brushes for the mural. She needed larger ones to paint walls; she cleaned the entire wall where the mural was to be painted, and she made two trips to Madrid to start speaking with the rape victims.

She realized that she needed to add a map to her findings, so she could pinpoint the exact locations where the rapes had taken place. She got a big map and put it on her office wall in the station. Her second realization came when she started taking notes in her interviews with the women. They all described the rapist as a very soft-spoken man, and polite. They described him as tall, over two meters, lean, and extremely strong. They guessed his weight as over 135 kilos, but those kilos had to be all muscle and not fat, since his overall build was slender. While not all the victims had seen his face, those who had

The Urge

stated he looked vaguely familiar to them, but just couldn't put a name with the face. Who was he that a number of women, from different locations, different experiences, and different education levels, thought that he looked familiar? Was he someone famous?

As her interviews broadened into areas beyond the center of Madrid, to Salamanca, Guadalajara, and Seville, she made another discovery. Looking at calendars and the dates when the rapes had occurred, she made a connection that the Madrid rapes occurred on nights during the week, but all the rapes outside Madrid occurred on weekends. If the rapist lived in Madrid, he would be working somewhere probably in Madrid during the week; therefore, he would rape his victims in Madrid. But if he lived in Madrid, on the weekends he could go to other cities or towns outside of Madrid and rape there.

Marielena took up the rest of her office wall with an enlarged chart with the date, the day of the week, the victims' names, the exact location where the rape occurred, and the city in which it occurred. During her interviews with the victims, she had started making a rough sketch of what the rapist might look like. She showed the sketch to each of the victims, and they agreed that it almost looked like him, but "not quite". They did agree on four things about his looks. He had a receding hairline, brown or dark hair, a small brown mustache, and "strange-looking" eyes. Well, at least she had something to go on. She also had the one sample of DNA from the victim in Seville. If it was the same rapist, it was a start. If not, it was an outlier that wouldn't fit with the rest of the victims. It couldn't be a copycat, because the Madrid police had not published all the facts which they had concerning the rapist. They especially hadn't released the fact that he had knocked out victims in order to escape.

Chapter 8

In the meantime, Marielena was making progress with the mural. It was going faster than she had anticipated and would be finished within the next month. Her hard work over the last two years sketching in the village streets had paid off. She had more than enough sketches and was rapidly enlarging them and transferring them to the town hall wall. She had grown to love San Anton, her adopted hometown now, and that love showed in her work. As she started to paint, the colors, textures, and structures she loved seemed to jump from her mind to paintbrush, palette, then to the wall. Several of the city council members had come by to inspect and had complimented her on her work. Even the Elliot villa, she still thought of it like that, looked regally down on the old town from its perch on the hill above the train station and river in the landscape view of the entire village. This landscape view took up about one-third of the entire mural. She thought again of her dear friend, Margarita. Even though she was dead and buried, she would always be a friend. In some small way, this mural would be another memorial to her and her memory. Yes, Marielena's real portrait of Margarita now hung in the Prado and showed the world what a beautiful woman Margarita had been. That portrait commission of Margarita had been the first commission that she had obtained in this village. It had been her real beginning in this village and her friendship with Margarita was her first real friendship there. She would never forget that friendship. It had meant a great deal to her. She vowed to make this mural the best painting she could accomplish, just as that portrait had been the best she could paint of her dear friend.

That very afternoon, as she went to work at the police station, another rape was reported. This time it had occurred closer to San Anton. This rape had occurred in the old town area of Toledo. Marielena

The Urge

realized that the rapist was coming closer to her own police district. The rape had occurred during the past weekend but hadn't been reported until Wednesday. Marielena had no trouble contacting this victim because she was living so close. The victim's name was Joanna Pazo, a young girl of twelve. Her parents had sent her out to buy bread at the overnight deli, but she hadn't returned right away. It should have taken her only fifteen minutes to make that trip. As expected, the worried parents had immediately called the police. The police found her quickly, but she was in such a state of fear, anxiety, and shock that she could hardly speak. She was also suffering a great amount of pain. This time the rapist had made a grievous error. He had raped a virgin. Besides shock and pain, she was losing copious amounts of blood. The rape had torn her tissues, both inside and outside. The victim had been admitted to the local hospital for examination and surgical repair. Her parents were devastated by her condition and insisted that the rapist be found immediately. When Marielena was finally allowed to speak to Joanna, with her mother present, the girl described a scenario consistent with the M.O. of the rapist which Marielena was trying to find. And, when the girl looked at the sketch which Marielena had made, she identified the man in the sketch as her rapist by screaming, "That's him. That's the man! No - no - no! Don't let him get me again!" Her mother took her in her arms to comfort her as the nurse-on-call rushed to get a sedative. Both the nurse and the attending physician were afraid that the girl would thrash around enough to rip the newly placed stitches. Indeed, as she slipped into unconsciousness, she seemed to be fighting her attacker all over again. Marielena waited as the girl's mother held her in her arms until she finally slept. Marielena couldn't understand how any man could have taken advantage

Chapter 8

of such a beautiful young girl - a child. It was the worst case Marielena had experienced. The man had to be a monster! It made her even more determined to find him and have him arrested and prosecuted.

When she returned to the police station in San Anton, she added the information to her chart and her map. What a poor, unfortunate, little girl, thought Marielena. We just have to catch this animal! Looking at her chart, she knew that, not only had the rapist's area increased, but the frequency was also increasing. She included this rape into the "outside Madrid" findings; however, when she considered the short drive or short train or bus ride between the two cities, she wondered if it should really fall within the scope of the Madrid rapes.

The next afternoon after working at the police sttion, she returned to the town hall to work on the mural. She was delighted that she was almost finished. The completion had been sped up by her no longer having to spend extra time each morning traveling to Toledo to take lessons with Master Chow. It was so much easier just going to work at the police station each morning and doing art in the afternoons. She thought fondly of Master Chow and had followed his advice to practice the various pattern executions of her martial arts training whenever she returned home. They seemed to come more easily to her every day - almost second nature. Her thoughts turned again to the poor little girl in the Toledo hospital. She wondered if the child had taken martial arts classes, would she have been able to avoid the rapist? Probably not, as she had only just turned twelve and was very petite. What if all women had an opportunity to be trained in martial arts self-defense? She couldn't help but feel that at least some would benefit and perhaps avoid being raped. She prayed that she herself would never

The Urge

have to put her training to practice. Thanks to her wonderful husband, she would at least have a fighting chance against any attack. Oh, how she loved Diego for loving her and looking out for her safety.

~ ~

Chapter 9
Marielena's Sister, Eva

Marielena sat at her desk and pondered the growing list of rape victims, women whose lives had been changed forever. She shook her head and contemplated the life changes that she knew they would have to face. Emotions would run from regret to guilt, anger to sorrow, indecision to a decision about everyday activities, fear to determination, and concern about themselves and their friends, relatives, and neighbors. Their lives had been changed by one event. Not only would they have their life changed, but everyone close to them would experience a change.

She remembered when Eva, her second to oldest sister had been raped. At the time Marielena had only been ten, but she'd been old enough to see that it wasn't just Eva who had been affected, their entire family had suffered.

Eva had been found eventually by her father, the police, and her fiancée. She was almost incomprehensible, bloody, and bruised. Eva had been

The Urge

expected by her family that evening. She worked in a leather factory several kilometers from home, but she hadn't come home as anticipated. The sun had set hours after her usual arrival time. The night was dark with no moon nor stars, just lots of clouds trying to brew up a storm. The day had been exceedingly hot and unusually humid. While the factory had lots of fans, there was no air conditioning which meant that she usually came home completely exhausted as well as famished. When she didn't arrive, they had assumed she had taken some overtime hours. The factory where she was employed had been very busy during the last few months and Eva had often worked extra hours, even extra shifts. She and her fiancée were trying to save money for their upcoming wedding. Eva's wedding dress, on order, was breathtakingly beautiful, but more expensive than she had planned. All the family said Eva would be the loveliest bride that they would ever see, but it was costly.

Normally when Eva worked extra hours, she'd call the family. That night there had been no call. Most of the other siblings had gone on to bed, including Marielena. She had just begun to drift off to sleep. Not quite though. She could hear her parents in the next room discussing Eva and why she hadn't come home. She heard them decide to call the factory. When they did, they discovered that Eva wasn't there. Secondly, they decided to call her boss, whom they knew from church. In fact, he had helped Eva get her job as a friendly favor. When they called him, he informed them that Eva had not been given extra hours and had left the factory on time. She should be home. They discussed what to do next and called Eva's fiancée. He hadn't heard anything from her either, but he would come over immediately. From the tone of her parents' voices, Marielena knew for sure something was wrong. By then she had lost even the remotest

Chapter 9

interest in going to sleep. Where was her sister? What had happened?

She heard Eva's fiancée arrive and, after some discussion, her dad went next door to wake their neighbor. He and Señor Sanchez had called the police who arrived at the door within a few minutes. The police, her father, the neighbor, and Eva's fiancée were going to walk to the factory, stop in every place that remained open, and try to find Eva. By this time Marielena was wide awake. She got up to sit and wait with her mother. As time passed, her oldest sister and her brother had awakened and joined them in their kitchen. The four of them sat and waited for two hours. More time passed until finally, the door opened.

Her father, their neighbor – Señor Sanchez, Eva's fiancée, the police officers, and Eva entered. Eva's clothes had been torn, her face and arms were bloody, and her face was severely bruised and starting to swell. She had been found only three blocks from the factory. Not only had she been beaten, but she'd been raped. They had stopped by only long enough to update her mother. Eva was being taken to the hospital to be examined.

Marielena's mother broke down sobbing at the sight of her daughter. She kept repeating, "Why, why?"

Eva told them, "I couldn't get away. I tried. I fought, but he was too strong. I tried to scream, but there was no one around to hear me. He held my hands behind my back. I couldn't break loose. He groped me. He raped me. I'm so sorry. I'm so sorry."

Her fiancée asked, "What are you sorry for? Did you know this guy? Did you flirt with him? What did you do that you say you're sorry?"

Eva answered, "I tried to get away!"

The Urge

"Evidently, not hard enough."

"I did! I did!"

At that point, one of the police officers took Eva's fiancée by the arm and motioned him to go with him outside the front door. Marielena could hear through the semi-open door as the police officer told Eva's fiancée, "Sir, she's had a hard enough time tonight without you trying to make her feel guilty. It's been my experience that rape isn't the victim's fault. Right now, she needs compassion, not more abuse." The rest of his comments were spoken so softly that Marielena couldn't hear them. After several more minutes, Eva's fiancée walked back into the room, went to Eva, and apologized to Eva, saying, "Please forgive me. I was so upset myself that I've been very unfeeling for what you've gone through."

This had been the first time that Marielena had been exposed to a rape victim, but her memories were so vivid that it seemed but yesterday that it had occurred.

Other memories flashed back from the past. She remembered hearing Eva and her mother crying together in each other's arms after Eva returned from the hospital. They expressed relief that Eva wasn't going to be pregnant. She remembered her father's anger at not being able to find out who had despoiled his daughter. She remembered lengthy discussions he and her mother had held with police officers who also expressed anger over not being able to find Eva's assailant. She remembered the fear her parents had concerning her and her other sister; their multiple warnings about not walking alone, keeping away from dark streets and alleys, and calling to inform them about their whereabouts. She remembered Eva being afraid to go out after dark by herself. Most of all, she

Chapter 9

remembered the sight of Eva on the night of the rape.

All these memories - too much. No, rape doesn't just affect the victim. Rape affects the entire family and the close friends and relatives of the victim. Rape is an offense against humanity.

Marielena again thanked God, as she had done right after Eva's ordeal, that Eva's boyfriend had been understanding and reassuring of his love, that Eva's marriage had allowed her to resume her life encouraging her to go on in a positive direction, and that Eva had been able to put the experience into her past. Many women, who experienced rape, were not as fortunate.

As Marielena looked at the list of rape victims on her office wall again, she felt more determined than ever to find the rapist. Maybe she hadn't been able to put her sister's rapist away, but she felt internally driven and personally motivated to put this current rapist away. No woman should have to go through what her sister had gone through. No family should have to have a family member suffer through this as her family had suffered.

~ ~

Chapter 10
The Mural

At last, the mural was finished. The city council members were thrilled with the result and decided, not only to have a proper dedication ceremony but to publicize the fact that their hometown artist had "out-painted" herself and was being honored as the creator of this splendid mural. The local newspaper reporters, as well as reporters from Toledo and Madrid, were invited to the celebration.

Marielena was introduced and had her pictures taken with the council members who spoke glowingly of her artistic abilities and her hard work. She herself spoke a few words at the dedication about her love of her newfound, hometown. She described how her sketches of the town and memories of her friend Margarita, now deceased, had prompted her to work hard to portray the town as a peaceful and close-knit community of people dedicated to the arts and to each other.

Many in the audience, including Señora Santiago,

The Urge

clapped loudly at her words. Diego beamed with love and pride at his wife. While her artistic passion, talent, and vocation were touted at the celebration, no one bothered to mention that she also worked for the local police force. It was mentioned by the mayor that her artistic abilities had become noticed by the community for her painting of Margarita Elliot, the former Miss Spain and Miss World - a now-deceased member of their village. He also made it a point to proudly proclaim that this painting by Marielena was now hanging prominently in the Prado Art Museum in Madrid. Marielena blushed at all the praise amid flashing cameras that were photographing her and her mural.

A couple of days later as newspapers carried her story and photograph to the far corners of Spain, an art professor at the Carreras Universitarias de Bellas Artes in Madrid saw them and decided his students might learn from this acclaimed artist about how to advance their budding art careers. He decided to invite Marielena to come to Madrid to demonstrate and to help lecture his classes for a week. She was Spanish, local, and now very much well-known. She was the kind of guest speaker who could improve his students' knowledge. She looked like an intelligent young woman who would be willing to share her expertise. From her remarks about her deceased friend, Margarita, she would be caring enough to speak with students. The fact that her art was hanging in the Prado alone was enough for the students to hang on her every word. She was perfect! He decided to send a letter to her via the city council in San Anton; and, if she would be willing, he would invite her to share her expertise with his students.

Two days later one of the city council members contacted Marielena and told her that a letter

Chapter 10

addressed to her had arrived. It was from someone at the Carreras Universitarias de Bellas Artes en Madrid. At least that was what the return address said.

Marielena had no idea what was going on, but at her earliest opportunity she went to the town hall and picked up the letter. When she opened it, she could hardly believe her eyes. She was invited by Professor Alejandro Villars Correao Castillo Bodega to come to the university to demonstrate her art and to lecture about what it is like to be a working and recognized, professional artist. He wanted his students to understand her background in terms of education, experience, and personal philosophy concerning art and being a professional artist. He also suggested she describe to them how to obtain commissions and how to make a living as an artist. He stated that he had seen the articles concerning the town hall mural and he knew that she had one of her paintings in the Prado. That alone, he proclaimed, was enough to make her an important enough person to talk to his art students.

Marielena was astounded, as well as deeply flattered. She wondered about how she would have felt had she experienced speaking to someone like herself when she was a student. Would it have changed how she looked at art for a professional career? Again, she heard her mother's voice coming to her from the past, saying, "You'll never be able to make a living as an artist." She remembered asking herself only two years ago, before the Elliot commission, if she would be able to make it on art alone without having another job to pay the bills. That seemed so far away. And, yet, it wasn't. Had she been lucky? Or had it been meant to be? What exactly could she tell the professor's students? They were setting out on the exact same pathway that she had chosen for herself. Speaking to young people about having an art career would be

The Urge

a challenge for her. How could she be encouraging, yet remain realistic in terms of what they would experience during their lifetimes? She knew that the many ups and downs, which she had experienced, needed to be explained. Being an artist was having a commitment to be your own being, not someone else. It meant developing your own style, regardless of current trends in the art world. You had to be true to only one person, yourself. How could she possibly express that in only one week?

As she reread the letter, she realized that the professor had considered her worthy enough that he had gone to the university board and together they were offering to pay for a hotel room for a week, giving her a per diem to purchase food wherever she wished, as well as paying her a one week's salary as a guest lecturer. The terms were quite generous. Before she could accept, she needed to speak to Diego. Her husband was also her boss. She'd need to take a one-week leave-of-absence from the police force, plus she'd need to be away from home and his company for that week. Her work about finding the serial rapist would also be on hold for a week - no talks with victims, no consultations with the Madrid police force, and no more work on any other projects. She pocketed the letter and went back to the police station.

She walked slowly back to the station and went into Diego's office to tell him about the offer. He looked up at her as she entered his office and, realizing from her facial expression that she had something of importance to share, he put down his pen and asked, "What's up?"

She sank down in the chair across the desk from him and said, "You could never guess what I'm being asked to do. In fact, I'm really astounded myself. You know the town council received a letter addressed to

Chapter 10

me and called me over to pick it up. Here it is." She opened her purse, extracted the letter, and pushed it across the desk to him.

He picked it up and looked at the return address on the envelope. "The Carreras Universitarias de Bellas Artes en Madrid?"

"Yes," she said. "They want me to come for a week to demonstrate and lecture. And they're not only willing to pay a salary, but to pay for my hotel and a per diem for my meals. They'll even make the hotel reservation for me as soon as I confirm that I'll come."

"A whole week?" Diego asked.

"Yes, but that means I'll have to be gone for a week from here, take a leave of absence, and not be working on finding the serial rapist. "Plus, it will be a week apart from you too."

"Oh, but what an honor."

"Yes, it is."

"How did they hear about you?"

"They read the newspaper articles about the town hall mural and how I was noticed for painting the portrait of Margarita in the Prado."

"My question is, do you want to do it?"

"I'm not sure really. I thought about it on the way over here, and I wondered what my art career would have been like if I had been given the opportunity to talk to a successful artist before I had finished my art education. Would it have made a difference to me? Would I have made different decisions? My mom, who wasn't an artist, told me not to become an artist. I became one anyway despite the difficulties. When I began this journey, I didn't realize just how tough it

The Urge

would be. Maybe if I speak to these students, they'll understand just how hard an artist's life really is."

"Sounds to me like you'd like to do it to discourage them"

"Not really. But someone needs to speak to them about the reality of making decisions that will affect your entire life. I guess maybe someone needs to encourage them, not discourage them. Being an artist is difficult, not impossible. If you want to become a professional artist, you need to approach it with a realistic idea of what serious impediments will impact your life. Unless you know 'the right people' who will open doors for you, you're on your own. There are some artists who are helped, but most are not. When you're on your own, only your own talent and hard work will determine how far you will go or how many accolades you will receive. Maybe I'm the one who can give these students a clear view of what to expect when they leave the security of the academic world and enter the real competitive world that awaits them. The longer I think about it, the more I think I need to do this."

Diego answered her, "If you want to do it, I will support you, 100 percent. I can allow you to take a one-week leave with no pay, since they are willing to pay you as you work there. My problem is different. As a husband, I'll be living without you for a week, but I've been on my own before, and I can manage. But I'll really miss you while you're gone."

Marielena stood up, walked around the desk, and kissed her husband saying, "I'll miss you too, dear; but I really feel that I need to do this. It's another step in my growth as an artist - sharing my knowledge and experiences."

Marielena left Diego's office, went into her own

Chapter 10

office, and called Professor Villars to finalize all the details. She gave him a choice of weeks when she could be available and told him her home phone number and address. He wouldn't have contacted the San Anton city fathers if he had already obtained this information. He let her know which week was best, where she would be staying in Madrid, and where on the university campus she could meet him when she arrived. Later as she reviewed their conversation, she realized that this would definitely be a new experience for her - lecturing to art students instead of being an art student.

~ ~

Chapter 11
Marielena Goes to the University

Two weeks later Marielena met Professor Villars. He was such a pleasant man who was thoroughly concerned for his students' futures that Marielena was immediately put at ease with him. She explained to him, as she had to her husband, the reasons she had accepted his offer to become a guest lecturer and demonstrator. Hopefully, she could present a realistic view of life as a working artist to these prospective future artists. She stated that she was both honored and humbled to be asked to participate in his students' education. She promised that she would do her very best to live up to his high expectations of both her artistic abilities and her success as an educator.

Since Diego was busy working and Madrid was so close, she had taken the train and a taxi straight to the university. Professor Villars walked her to the nearby hotel where the university had engaged a room for her to stay during the week that she would be working there. She checked in and walked back with him to the university to meet with the students who would be

The Urge

"her" students during the coming week. The classes assigned to her were all second-year art students pursuing a variety of art degrees. They were at an age that Professor Villars had thought might be best influenced by her "words of wisdom", as he phrased it. She had agreed with his decision. She remembered from her years as an art student that during her second year of studies she had vacillated in her mind about whether an art career was a goal that she really wanted. Again, her mother's words haunted her. It was as though she heard her mother say, "You'll never be able to make a living at art".

The first afternoon was basically introductions and orientation for both her and the students. She looked into their eager and anticipatory faces and knew she had made the right decision about being there with them. She knew that, like these students, she had a deeply rooted dedication and love of art. This shared passion for art made her fall in love with the students and with the task set before her. She described to them where, and especially how, she had grown up. She told them how she had displeased her mother with her choice of career and how, because of finances, she had chosen to go to art schools in Barcelona. While that school wasn't as prestigious as where they were going to college, it offered her a minuscule scholarship. Afterward, she apprenticed herself to a well-known artist who also worked in Barcelona. She went through with the students the progression of media which she had studied, how much she liked some and disliked others, with her memories of trying to decide which medium she would specialize in and why. After her apprenticeship of two years, she went to Rhonda, to try her luck as a professional artist. While there, she stated, she had experienced difficulties in finding a reasonably priced place to live, as well as making enough money to feed herself. She continued with a

Chapter 11

description of working first in a bar, then later in a small store to try to make ends meet. She said at that point in her life, she could only work part-time at her art and was frustrated by the news that many of her fellow students, who had tried to be full-time artists were making it but were living at almost poverty level and also taking other jobs. A few of the lucky ones had found sponsors or patrons who guaranteed them an income large enough that they could be full-time artists. She cautioned the students that the same scenario would face them in the future. She told them that her problem had been that she was not the only artist living in Rhonda and all the artists there were having the same problems and living in the same circumstances.

One of the students raised her hand and asked, "How did you solve this problem for yourself?"

Marielena said, "It took a lot of courage, but I put money aside, although I could barely feed myself with what money I had. When I thought I'd saved enough to live for two months without any income, I left Rhonda and moved to San Anton, a suburb of Toledo. From what I had read and had been told, I chose that area because it seemed to be a more affluent area with greater populations in close-by Madrid and Toledo. I thought I might have more success in a more populated area."

The students leaned forward in their seats in anticipation of her continued story. A male student raised his hand and asked, "Did it help, and, if so, would you encourage us to do the same thing?"

"Yes, it did help. But - something else helped - a little luck. As I sketched in the village, I was approached by a man who commissioned me to paint his wife for a significant amount of money. Or at least it seemed

The Urge

a lot of money at the time. Remember, I had been living on practically nothing. Anything in comparison would have seemed to be a huge windfall." Marielena walked to the chalkboard, picked up a piece of chalk, and wrote the word "commissions" on the chalkboard. She then asked the students, "What do you understand about this word?"

Several students volunteered answers to her question. She nodded thoughtfully as each answer was given to her query. She quietly waited for any more answers until all the students had had an opportunity to think about and respond to the question. Finally, after several minutes of silence, she said, "I know from your responses that you believe that this word is almost 'magic' to artists. Let me assure you that 'commissions' may not be the answer to all your desires as an artist. Let me explain." She wrote down four numbers under the word "commissions" so that she could fill in more information as she continued to make her points.

"Number 1. You must protect yourself. You may finish a commission and your client may not like it and refuse to finish paying you for all your hard work. Therefore, always have a written contract." She wrote "written contract" in the space beside the number 1. She said, "In your contract, you must clearly state everything in detail."

She continued, "Half of the price must be paid up-front, and that half should not be refundable. After all, when you have accepted a commission, you forfeit your time that you could be working on other things, many of which might be more profitable to you than the commission. You'll need income to live on, so be sure the amount that you quote for the commission is not only large enough to cover the supplies you'll need to do it, but also your living expenses. Also, be sure to

Chapter 11

add in extra money for any unseen expenses which you might incur. The last half of the commission price is due at the end of the commission when the client takes possession of it. Be sure to have it in writing and signed by both you and your client to include in this contract that, if they do not like it, they have not only forfeited the down-payment, but also the artwork itself; and that artwork becomes your property to do with as you wish. That's another reason to add extra to the cost because you'll have to have a way to continue with your life if the client rejects it. You've just spent part of your life working on something no one wants. But you want it because you have blood, sweat, and tears in it. After a few seconds, waiting for her words to sink in, she added, "Usually a commission is of such a determined subject or so specific in its nature that no one else will want it so be prepared for that scenario. You may never find anyone that wants it, and you may be sitting on a 'red herring'." There was absolute silence in the classroom as the students digested that fact.

Finally, another student asked, "What's number 2?"

Marielena wrote on the chalkboard by #2, "Hard work". She stated, "You will never work as hard in your life as on a commission. Remember, in a commission you're not painting for yourself. You're painting for someone else and their idea of what 'they want' might not be exactly the same as 'what you think they want', or 'what you want' for that artwork. Also, you might disagree with your client on two other things: whether the commission is good or not, or exactly when it is finished. Be very careful you know what your client wants, or your time will be wasted. Remember, when the client accepts the commissioned artwork, it is finished. He or she must also realize that the acceptance states to everyone, that the artwork

The Urge

doesn't need any more work on it."

"And, number three?" spoke up another student.

"Number 3 is that there may be an ulterior motive behind the commission. A fellow artist I knew in Rhonda accepted a commission that sounded very good at the time. This artist worked in landscapes and the client wanted him to paint a very large canvas of a landscape of a place that she and her family had seen on a vacation. The spot they showed the artist where the painting would be hung was over their oversized fireplace. When my artist friend completed the painting after a solid month of working on it, the client and her daughter stated, 'Oh, that's perfect'.

"Three weeks later they called the artist, demanded that he return their money, and said they didn't like the painting. They threatened, in spite of the contract, to sue the artist in court if their money wasn't refunded. After consulting a lawyer, my artist friend refunded their money, but insisted, that by contract, the painting was now his. When he went to pick up the painting, there was another huge painting hanging over the fireplace.

My friend asked about it and was told, 'We only wanted something large enough for this space and we like this painting so much better than the one which you did'. It proved to him that their commission was a lie and he'd spent all his time on painting a canvas they really didn't want. Their final comments showed not only what little regard they had for artists and my artist friend's work, but that they had not been truthful from the very beginning about why they wanted the artist to paint the landscape. All they wanted was to "fill a wall". They were just using him until they found something they liked better."

All the students expressed amazement at that

Chapter 11

comment, she wrote beside the #3 on the chalkboard, "if the commission looks too good to be true, it may be a hoax". She turned around to face the class and said, "I should have been warned about the commission which I accepted in San Anton. I hadn't been in San Anton long enough to develop a clientele for any commissions, but I was approached by an offer that wasn't realistic. One needs to be sure to establish yourself in a community before accepting any commissions, no matter how good they look. I was too eager and under-educated in terms of artists and commissions. Be sure to remember my words to you and judge an offered commission carefully before you accept it, even with a contract."

The professor asked, "And, number four?"

Marielena laughed and said, "That's the easy one. Don't rely on commissions. Usually, they're few and far between. If you continue on your path to becoming an artist, paint for yourself, develop your own style, remain true to who you are, and work hard. If you are truly meant to be an artist, the world will find you and validate you as an artist. They do that by purchasing your artworks." As she wrote "don't rely on commissions for your validation or income", the students gave her a standing ovation.

And, therefore it was with applause that she ended her first afternoon as a guest speaker.

~ ~

Chapter 12
Marielena Continues at the University

As Marielena left the university and went back to her hotel, she felt a warm sense of comradery with the students. Her first day had gone well and she wanted to eat at the hotel that night and spend the rest of the evening preparing for the following morning. She was planning to discuss the painting in the Prado with the students, showing them her initial sketches, which she had brought with her, and showing pictures of the finished painting. In the afternoon, the professor had arranged a field trip to the Prado so that the students could see Marielena's actual canvas "The Spanish Beauty". Marielena would fill in the students about Margarita's life. She planned to describe Margarita's rise in fame to become Miss Spain and Miss World and why the museum had wanted to have the painting in its collection. It would be a full day.

And it was. The students loved hearing her story about the painting, its inception, and its execution. The story about her dear friend, Margarita, had brought a tear to some of the female students' eyes. Then she

The Urge

was asked how the painting had been purchased by the museum.

Marielena had replied, "Unbeknownst to me, one of my friends contacted the museum because he knew some of the curators. When they heard of it and who the person in the portrait was, they decided it was a historic painting which might possibly be one which they'd want in the museum".

"And then what happened?" Asked one of the students.

"They came and looked at it and decided to buy it."

"I thought it was a commissioned portrait. Didn't the person who commissioned it want it?"

"No. Remember when we discussed the word 'commission' yesterday? My first point was to protect yourself so that, if the painting was unwanted at the end of the painting, the painting becomes the property of the artist. Well, that's what happened to 'The Spanish Beauty'. Yes, both the subject of the painting, who was a Spanish beauty, and the painting, which I named 'The Spanish Beauty', were unwanted by her husband. After her death, the painting was unwanted by both her husband's family, because of sad memories of their daughter-in-law, and her family, because they couldn't afford it. Everyone refused to pay the last half of my commission fee, thereby relinquishing total rights of the painting to me, the artist."

"Wow", "Cool", "Sweet", "Super", and "Yeah" were some of the students' replies to her answer.

"Remember you have to protect yourself," answered Marielena.

"Perhaps you should fill them in on what happened next," said Professor Villars.

Chapter 12

Marielena smiled and said, "That's tomorrow's lesson."

The students groaned.

At that, the professor reminded the students they were to return after lunch, meet at the front door of the art building, and leave on their field trip at four o'clock. Promptly at four, they were provided with one of the university buses to go to the Prado Museo, and, as they left, she could hear the excited whispers of the students as they were questioning what this fabulous painting of hers looked like. As the students left the bus to enter the museum, Professor Villars helped shepherd all the students to the location of her painting and then stepped back to allow her to describe it in detail and how it was conceived.

Marielena stood to one side and told the students to analyze what she had done in designing, composing, and executing the painting. She reminded them to keep in mind that the subject or model was an important personage. After about twenty minutes she asked what they had learned.

Several students remarked about the size of the canvas and the full-frontal view of the woman being turned only slightly to her right. One student said that the painting reminded him of large works by Velasquez. Another student said the painting reminded her of the paintings which she had seen of kings, especially one of Napoleon in his formal ermine robe. Still, more students said, since the subject here was dead, the painting somehow reminded them of Goya's firing squad which was done during the Spanish Civil War. Others asked if the objects in the painting and the background had any significance.

Marielena stated that when she had been commissioned, her patron had stated his love of the

The Urge

artworks by Van Eyck where all objects in the painting had significance and the background also had importance, but to a lesser degree. Her statement led the students into a lively discussion comparing "The Spanish Beauty" to Van Eyck's works.

Soon it was time for them to catch their bus back to the university and end their class for the day. On the ride back to the university many of the students continued their discussion. Marielena felt the entire day had been worthwhile and so did the professor when they consulted back at the university.

The next day – her third day with the students, Marielena had taken not only her sketches and photos for "The Spanish Beauty", but she had also taken her sketches and photos for the town hall mural in San Anton. As she entered the classroom, every single one of the students was already in their seats in anticipation of her lesson.

She began her lesson by talking about the difference between painting on canvas, even a large one like "The Spanish Beauty" and painting a huge wall-sized mural in a building. She followed with a comparison of being commissioned by a government authority versus being commissioned by a single individual, meeting the expectations of a large group versus an individual. Again, she reminded them that an artist must be sure you receive in writing, exactly how they, singular or plural, want the mural. Of course, the subject of the mural is dictated by its purpose, especially such a large mural. She showed them photos of murals in many European cities which she had collected. Some were political and propaganda in nature, some were bucolic and peaceful, and some showed great pride in the famous sites of the area surrounding the building where the mural was located. She explained that the city fathers of San Anton had great pride in their

Chapter 12

community and had wanted her to display the famous sites and scenery of their area - sort of a combination of peaceful scenery and famous sites.

Digressing a little, she described how, when she had moved to the San Anton area, she had spent a lot of time learning about her new hometown. She had spent hours going through the town, sketching, and painting the landmark buildings and scenery. Marielena cautioned them, "You need to learn your area. People who have lived there all their lives will immediately see if you paint or sketch it incorrectly. If you want to build a reputation in the area, this will make or break you. And word of mouth is the best form of advertisement for an artist. You must 'get it right'. It depends less on your style than on your exactness. For example, if you're painting the local church where everyone has been baptized, married, and buried, you should make it look like that church. Otherwise, no one will buy it. Also remember, practice makes perfect - so, you'll do it over and over again. Each time will be better. Keep in mind, that while you're painting for yourself, if you're a professional and want to sell, you need to keep your patrons in mind. Even if you're not a realistic painter, but an abstract painter, your patrons must feel a relationship to what you're painting. Usually, murals in public buildings aren't abstract, but that doesn't mean you shouldn't know your area and what the people there want."

"Is that what you did?" asked one of the students.

"Yes. When the city fathers knew of my successful painting in the Prado and knew of other paintings which I was selling in town, they decided to commission me to paint the mural in their city hall. Truthfully, it was an easy commission to accept because most of the groundwork had already been done. The hours of sketching and painting around the town made the job

The Urge

much easier. The hardest part was deciding which of my sketches they wanted me to incorporate into the mural. A few of my sketches were at a different angle than they wanted. I had to go back and do them over until I received their approval.

Marielena laid out all her sketches and small watercolors of San Anton sites so the students could look at them. She purposely didn't lay out just the ones that had ended up in the mural. Then she had the students after they had looked at all of them, decide which ones they would have chosen for a mural. A lively discussion erupted, which lasted for most of the rest of the morning.

After a lunch break, she finally showed them photos of the completed mural and moved the chosen sketches into their positions in the actual mural. She enlightened them about why the city fathers had chosen those particular sketches over the others. Many of the students made comments about how they would have felt after having some of the sketches rejected. Some students agreed with the selections and others didn't. Marielena reiterated the problems that may arise due to potential differences of opinion when one is working for others in commission artwork.

After discussing the subjects of the mural, she described how walls in buildings need to be cleaned and prepared for mural painting. She stated, "When painting on canvas, all you need to do is gesso it once or twice, perhaps sanding it down between layers, because you're starting on a clean surface, but that isn't the case when you're painting on the walls of a building, especially an older building that has seen many people come and go. People, whether they know it or not, release oils, carbon dioxide, and sweat that goes into the air and land on the walls. In painting a mural, the surface must be thoroughly cleaned before

Chapter 12

any paint is applied. If not, no matter how you choose to paint this surface, the paint must adhere to the walls and stay there, probably for a long time with a mural. Oils and other 'dirty things' on the walls will ultimately cause the paint to pull away, sometimes taking part of the wall with it. The mural will be totally ruined. The differences between painting a mural with today's paints versus painting a mural in Michelangelo's and de Vinci's times is different. They used fresco, a means of putting the pigment in the plaster itself. Today's murals have more permanence because our paints are stronger, especially acrylic paints with a plastic base and they are 'on' the wall, not 'in' the wall."

The entire afternoon flew by. Seldom did Professor Villar interrupt her, and Marielena knew from his few comments and his facial expressions that he was pleased with her presentation. She also knew from the students' questions and polite responses that she had accomplished her goals of encouraging them and helping them.

At the end of this third day, she said to the students, "We still have two more days to work together, so I would like to give you some homework for tomorrow and Friday. I want you to plan both a painting for tomorrow and plan a mural for Friday. Bring in a canvas which we will work on tomorrow. On Friday, bring in sketches that could be incorporated into a mural and a sketch of what the finished mural might look like. I know that at this point this is sort of an open-ended assignment, so I'll make it more difficult. First, we will get numbers from one to four for each of you." Walking around the classroom, she numbered each student.

When she was finished giving them each a number, she stated, "All #1's will do a portrait of a woman; all #2's will do a portrait of a man; all #3's will do a portrait of a cat, and all #4's will do a portrait of

The Urge

a dog." Some of the students groaned, and others cheered. She added, "If you wish, those of you doing people may paint each other". That comment made many students smile.

The next two days flew by with all the students busy at work. Marielena and the professor circulated around the classroom critiquing and helping students where needed. The professor thanked Marielena and collected the finished students' products. At the end of Thursday, several students approached the professor and expressed their desire to hold a small party for Marielena at a local bar not far from her hotel on Friday evening to thank her for all her help. The professor passed the invitation on to Marielena but said with regret that he himself had another commitment on Friday evening and could only be there with her and the students for a short time. He thanked her profusely and suggested that she accept the students' invitation - which she did. The students and she were happy that she'd accepted, not only the job of working with them but that she'd celebrate with them at a "going away party".

Thus, the last two days of her teaching assignment went by quickly. Thursday evening in her hotel, she packed up all her sketches, photos, and clothes. She'd be taking the train back to Toledo and San Anton on Saturday morning, and, with a party on Friday evening, she needed to be ready to leave since she wasn't sure how long the party would last.

~ ~

Chapter 13
The Celebration

Marielena met the students and the professor at the designated bar that Friday evening. Truly it was a celebration for all. The students were grateful for all her "words of wisdom" and considered her not only a good artist but also a mentor to them. The professor was delighted that his idea to have Marielena as a guest lecturer and demonstrator had been supported by the university and that it had been very beneficial to his students. Marielena saw that her instincts had been correct in accepting the invitation to give back to younger, emerging artists. It seemed that her lectures had hit home with a number of the students. She, however, was anxious to return home the next day.

After having one drink with the group, Professor Vallis expressed his regrets about having to leave, thanked Marielena again for coming to the university to speak and demonstrate to "his kids," and left the bar. The students were having a good time, asking her for more information about painting, and the time passed quickly. Marielena soon realized she was

The Urge

a little tipsy and decided to order a sandwich and a salad. When it came, she acknowledged that she was even more hungry than she had thought. Some of the students were now drifting off, dancing, or carrying on personal conversations. Thanking them for a lovely party, Marielena concluded her evening celebration and prepared to go back to her hotel. Looking outside, she was astonished at how dark the city had become and how few streetlights were in this neighborhood.

Just after she paid her bill and left, she remembered Master Chow's instructions. She moved her purse to a cross-chest position, took out her car keys (even though she didn't have her car and wasn't driving), and put her keys in her right hand with the sharp edges extending beyond her fingers. She felt foolish but decided she'd rather be safe than sorry. Plus, Madrid was where she was, and Madrid was the center of the serial rapist's activities. Fortunately, she only had to walk four blocks to her hotel. When she got there, she'd be in for the night and be safe.

About the third block from the bar and a block from her hotel, the walkway passed the unlit entrance to an underground parking garage. She was just passing the entrance when a hand reached out of the darkness and grabbed her right shoulder. Another hand was reaching out for her mouth.

Master Chow's instructions came to her automatically. Stepping in close to her attacker, she reached out with her right hand and scratched her assailant's face with the sharp ends of her keys. She was immediately aware that there was no verbal response to the contact by her attacker which seemed very strange. As she looked at his face, she visualized the sketch that she had done of the serial rapist as described by his victims. She remembered them saying he looked familiar, and, at that instance, he

Chapter 13

seemed familiar to her too. But she really didn't have time to think about it anymore as her attacker grabbed her again, swinging her around. Her left arm smashed into the darkened street signpost and an excruciating pain radiated up into her shoulder and whole body as she heard a loud snap. She gasped. Now she knew she really had to fight. Again, she stepped in closer and brought her knee up into his crotch, connecting with a hard thump. As her assailant doubled over, she executed a quick turn and, kicking outward with all the force she could muster, sent a roundhouse kick into his face. She again connected with his head with a hard blow. As her assailant slumped to the ground, she ran as fast as she could to her hotel, threw open the door, and yelled to the clerk, "Call the police. I was just attacked a block from here." At that point, she slumped into one of the lobby chairs shaking like a leaf. The adrenaline rush of her fight had now left as fast as it had come. She was totally exhausted. Her arm reminded her where she was also injured. Thank God, Diego had insisted she take self-defense classes with Master Chow. She hated to think about what might have happened without those precious lessons. If she had only been on duty, she would have had her service revolver on her, but she hadn't been on duty and she hadn't really thought that lecturing at the university would require a gun, so she had left it in San Anton.

The police arrived in fifteen minutes and one of them she knew because they had met when she was interviewing the rape victims and making the sketches of the rapist. He stayed to talk to her while his partner called for backup and went to the place a block away from where she had been attacked. He came back, stating that there was no one there. He had the backup unit searching more thoroughly to see if any trace could be found of her attacker, asking

The Urge

house to house for information. It was obvious to both police officers that she was in a lot of pain and needed to go to the hospital. Both her police officer friend and she determined her left arm was broken and would have to be set. Rather than wait for an ambulance, her friend decided to take her to the hospital himself. As he loaded her into his cruiser, his partner had Marielena tell them all that had happened from the time she left the bar until when she arrived at her hotel. As Marielena recited the entire details of her attack and one police officer drove, the other took copious notes. Marielena pulled her cell phone from her purse and asked for help holding it while she called Diego to tell him about the attack and that she was on the way to a hospital. She had been in such a hurry to get away from the rapist that she hadn't tried to use her phone to call for police help. Even if she had taken the time to do so, she saw in her mind's eye how the rapist could have revived and pulled her into the dark parking garage to "finish the job" on her. No, she was better to have run one block to the hotel before calling for help. She felt bad she hadn't called her husband before this, but everything had been too busy before now.

Diego answered the phone almost immediately and the minute she heard his voice she started to cry. The police officer took her phone from her and filled Diego in on what had transpired. She could tell by the conversation that Diego was as upset as she was. The police officer stated that they were driving her to the hospital. After hanging up, the police officer informed Marielena that Diego was on his way to Madrid and would see her at the hospital.

When they arrived at the hospital, they were met with a long line of people waiting to be attended. There had been a ten-vehicle chain-reaction accident earlier in the evening on the major highway through Madrid.

Chapter 13

Marielena had to wait for two hours before seeing a doctor who set her arm. They were just finishing with her cast when Diego walked into the operating room. Her big handsome husband had never looked so good to her. He wrapped her in his arms and held her as she again began to cry.

She sobbed, "I'm so glad you had me study with Master Chow. What I learned saved me tonight. I love you so much."

"I love you too. Do you need any pain meds for that arm?"

"The doctor has already given me a packet of pain meds and they're in my purse. Are we going home now?"

"No, it's after midnight. Aren't you still checked in at the hotel for tonight? We'll stay there and go home in the morning. After all, you were going to come home tomorrow morning anyway."

~ ~

Chapter 14
Rapist's Recollections

He was angry and disgusted with himself. The morning after he had attacked the woman, he couldn't believe what had happened. He had watched her drinking and partying with the students. He had followed her several times during the week. He knew where she was staying and where it would be easy to attack her. He had chosen her and "the urge" had been so strong. How could a "little thing like her" have fought him as she had. None of his other targets had possessed the courage and strength to fight back. Where had he errored?

His crotch was sore and swollen. His face had a huge purple bruise on it where her foot had connected. He had been forced to use some old theatrical makeup to cover it so he could go to work. Furthermore, his mask was ruined. He would have to go and get another. He wondered if he should get the same mask or a different one. This mask had worked very well. The news reports had stated that, while all his victims who had seen his face stated that he looked familiar, none

The Urge

had recognized him. Fantastic! Stupid women! After some thought, he decided to buy a new mask just like his old one. Too bad the woman had something sharp in her hand and had cut the mask downward across the left cheek from eye to chin. It was definitely irreparable. He'd have to wait until he felt better to go searching for a new mask. In the meantime, he'd just have to control "the urge" the best way he could.

He went to work but left early claiming he had a horrible headache. He did. But not for the reason he told his boss. He claimed that he had drunk too much the night before and had a hangover. And - his boss was too stupid and believed him. He hadn't even looked closely at his face.

He stopped by the newsstand and bought a copy of the local paper, which described his attack on the woman and her resistance. As his eyes scanned the news report, he was gratified to know that the woman had not escaped unscathed. Her left arm was broken. The break must have occurred when he swung her into the street sign. He was happy he'd chosen the part of the street where the light was nonexistent. Maybe she hadn't realized he'd been wearing a mask and she had damaged it. As he read further into the news report, he saw that she had contacted the police. He figured she would. All of them did, or most of them at least. She had also gone to the university hospital. And there - what was that? He reread the sentences over, again and again, to really believe what he was reading. Here were the words - "there the woman's husband, Police Commissioner Diego Rivera, from Son Anton, had met her." The next sentence was even worse. "The woman would be returning to her part-time job as a police detective in the San Anton Police Force". She worked in the same police department as her husband.

Chapter 14

No wonder she had fought back.

No wonder she had the knowledge and skills to fend him off.

How could he have been so stupid as to choose a woman who was a policewoman?

How could he have known?

What should he do now?

He had to go on trying to placate "the urge" but be more discrete in his choice of victims. He had to act normal. For the time being, he couldn't go on the hunt for a victim until everything settled down. While he waited for that, in the meantime, he would search for another mask just like this first one.

~ ~

Chapter 15
In San Anton

The night was dark - so dark, windy, and almost cold. Marielena walked quickly from the bar to her hotel. Sounds of laughter, toasts to friends, and ribald jokes floated to her from the revelry at the bar which she had just left. Pausing, she was lost in deep thought, but she couldn't seem to remember what she was thinking about. She knew she had been thinking about being at home with her beloved Diego - such lovely and loving thoughts. As she continued walking, a cat strolled by her going in the opposite direction. It looked up at her, as if in anticipation of something - maybe a scratch under the chin or a pat on the head. Marielena stopped and looked down at the cat, but the cat seemed to be in a hurry and walked quickly away on its own mission, whatever that was. Maybe it was hoping to get some nice little tidbit from under the outside tables which flanked the bar's front or maybe a choice morsel from the trash bin that Marielena had just passed. Regardless, Marielena found herself continuing in her walk - past apartment buildings, a

The Urge

vacant lot, and multiple parked cars, some on each side of the roadway. She passed several barely lit and dark openings to underground parking areas. She somehow knew she had to avoid those areas, but she couldn't remember why. She felt like she had walked several kilometers. Why so far? Why was it so dark? Her head hurt and her body felt so tired. It almost felt numb. Surely, she'd reach her destination soon. But how soon? She tried to pull her collar up against the cold, but it seemed as if her collar had gotten stuck under the front of her coat. She couldn't understand how that had happened. She tried to remember when she'd put on her coat. Had someone helped her? Why was she so alone?

She reached an alleyway between two apartment buildings and was ready to turn the corner to take a shortcut to her hotel when a hand reached out and grabbed her. She struggled with her assailant. She raised her hand and tried to throw her whole arm sideways in an attempt to push him away. She tried turning her body and, especially her legs, to one side. She found all motion blocked. Looking up she found a smiling face very near hers and heard a voice saying, "You can't get away." She thrashed and jerked, but she found herself unable to move. She broke out in a sweat; she struggled with all her might, and she found herself totally helpless. It wasn't a pleasant feeling.

The voice again spoke to her, "I'll not hurt you. Don't fight me. It will be over very soon. Just let me have you."

Marielena moaned, "No, no! Leave me alone. -- No. No. Noooooooooooo!"

She awoke to find Diego lying beside her, trying to calm her, and saying, "It's OK. It's over. I've got you. It's only a dream. You poor thing, you're shaking like a

Chapter 15

leaf. There. There. It's OK, Marielena. You're at home. You're safe. No one can get you. I'm here."

Marielena realized she'd been fighting, not an assailant, but the sheets, which were wrapped around her, especially her legs, preventing her from moving. The bed was soaking wet from her perspiration. Her arm, in its cast, seemed so heavy that she could barely lift it. No wonder she hadn't felt like she could move. Another night since she had been attacked. Another night of nightmares.

Within minutes she realized that her subconscious was still trying to save her from the attack which had happened days ago. Poor Diego. He was living through these episodes just like she was. He was trying to help her in every way he could. It was similar to how her whole family had tried to help her sister, Eva.

The past week had been spent trying to make sense of what had happened in Madrid. Thank God Diego had made sure she had taken those martial arts classes. They had enabled her to handle the real attack, but a nightly reenactment of that attack or a different version of that attack made her feel helpless. Some days she realized her dreams were reenactment versions of other victims' attacks, from her memories of interviews with other victims. Regardless, they all seemed so real - until she woke up.

Physically her arm was helping nicely, but psychologically she wasn't doing as well. She could really empathize with the women she had been interviewing about this rapist. It was as though she herself had ended up being raped. She prayed she'd be able to get over it. She'd been so lucky. She hadn't actually been raped, but the fear was still there; and the "what ifs" continued to hound her. Obviously, she had memories that were with her both day and night,

The Urge

both consciously and unconsciously.

Diego was so good to her and was always there to comfort her. It seemed that this night's dream wasn't quite as bad as the preceding nights. If this is what she was living through and her assailant hadn't succeeded in raping her, how were the real victims of rape managing to live through the post-trauma?

After about an hour in Diego's arms, she managed to fall asleep. This time dreamless.

When she awoke the next morning, she realized how lucky she really was. She had been trained to protect herself; she had not been raped; she only had a broken arm; she had her job and could look forward to finding this rapist and other criminals and putting them away; and she had the most loving, kind, and understanding husband imaginable. For now, she had one main and immediate mission - which she was determined to complete - she had to catch this guy. No more victims and victims' families need to go through this horror.

~ ~

Chapter 16
Diego's Thoughts

Diego sat at his desk looking extremely tired. The cup of coffee in front of him was giving him enough of a caffeine high so he could get his work done. During the last week neither he nor Marielena had gotten much sleep. During the day Marielena seemed fine, but her nightmares persisted so that sleep and rest hours had been few and far between.

Every night Marielena would fall asleep fairly easily, but after about an hour or two she'd start moving restlessly. She'd turn. She'd moan. She'd try to strikeout. Ultimately, she'd wake, needing to be comforted and reassured that she was at home, safe, and loved. While last night's dreams had seemed less intense than previous nights, she had still thrashed, turned, and spoke out in her sleep. She had also seemed to resume her sleep more easily, and it had been a quiet sleep with no more dreams. He prayed in time these nightmares would disappear entirely. The doctor had offered her sleeping meds, but Marielena refused them. She firmly stated that she would cope

The Urge

with this on her own without "a crutch", as she called it.

During the daytime, he noticed a subtle difference in her. She had always been a very focused person, able to work tirelessly. What he saw now was an almost driven individual. He saw a determination take over her. She was attacking the problem of finding the rapist with a vengeance, totally obsessed with the idea that because she herself had been attacked, she personally needed to find the man and put him behind bars. She had spoken to him about how her sister, Eva, had been raped and she had been too young to do anything about it. He watched her as she went about this quest as if her life depended upon its outcome.

Earlier she had arranged maps; lists of location, dates, and victims; a list of characteristics of rapists; and a list of questions still to be answered plastered all over the walls of her office. She continued pouring through newspapers, and news reports on the television and calling other police stations looking for more victims. She was dedicating more and more of her time to her search.

The wonderful thing was she really was putting everything together. Her tenacity of ferreting out detail was making headway in the case. In the meantime, her artistic abilities were allowing her to "see" the perp in a way that other police officers had not or were not able to do.

Today she had seemed a lot calmer to him, but he was still worried about her. He guessed because he loved her so much and was so sensitive to her moods and thoughts, he himself might be obsessing too much over what she was going through. He was glad that she was throwing herself into her work. Maybe that might hasten her concern over herself. Her energies

Chapter 16

would be focused more on the other victims in the case.

He made up his mind, depending upon his own workload, to spend extra time working with her on the case. He knew she was better with the interviews of the victims, but there might be something else that he could do to help her. Maybe he could help her in another way that hadn't occurred to him until that moment. Maybe he could have someone else help her with the trauma of her attack.

Taking the last sip of his coffee and finishing the report he had been working on, between thinking of Marielena and his duties, he decided to go speak to Señora Santiago. She had always possessed a way of soothing Marielena, and she always had words of wisdom to give to both of them. Marielena thought the world of her and, since Marielena's own parents were gone, she would benefit from the contact with another woman her mother's age. He left Deputy Ortega in charge, left the station, and walked to the Señora's house.

He had hardly knocked on the door when Señor Santiago opened the door and flung her arms around him. "How is Marielena? Is everything OK?"

He quickly explained that Marielena was doing well physically, her arm was healing nicely, and she had insisted on returning to work. She seemed to be doing well there, but psychologically she couldn't seem to recover from the attack, and she was experiencing nightmares. He wondered if the Señora would come over and talk with Marielena. "I know she values your friendship. Maybe, because you've pretty well taken over as a mother figure to her, she would feel better if she talked with you. I can only do so much. Maybe she needs a woman to confide in."

The Urge

"Of course, I'll come. When do you think it would be wise to come? I think you've come to me in secret, so I won't tell her that you've asked me to come. I'll just come by. I think it might be better if I could talk to her alone. What do you think?"

"I agree with you. I think she would probably open up to you if you spoke to her alone. I'll find a way to work late this evening, send her home alone, and have you come at that time. I'll tell her to leave early so she can rest. You plan on coming over a las ocho (at eight) and I'll leave work an hour and a half later. You'll have about two hours alone than with her."

"Fantastic. I'll be there. I might bring some flan over. I made some this morning. See you later."

Diego left with a sense of relief.

Later that afternoon he went into Marielena's office and told her that he wanted her to go home early. He said that he knew she was tired and getting little sleep. He wanted her to take a nap and not worry about dinner. He was going to work late and would stop at El Belloto and bring carryout for both of them. Giving her a hug and kiss, he sent her home after she agreed that, yes, she was extremely tired.

True to her word, Marielena had just gotten home when Señora Santiago knocked on the door. Both women hugged and kissed both cheeks of the other. Señora Santiago said, "I've been worried about you and, having baked a flan this morning and seeing you come home early, I thought I'd bring part of the flan over for your dinner."

"That's so kind of you," said Marielena. "How have you been? It's been a while since we've been able to talk. Diego will miss seeing you though. He said he had to work late tonight. Please come in and sit

Chapter 16

down. Can I get you something to drink? I have some lemonade in the refrigerator."

"Oh, that would be nice."

Marielena went to the kitchen and brought out a tray with two tall glasses of iced lemonade. Setting the tray on the table she said, "I'm sorry to have worried you, but really I'm OK and I've gotten over the attack."

"Really? You look about as tired as I've ever seen you. Are you sleeping well?

Marielena paused for a minute and answered, "Not really. I keep having nightmares. I guess I'm reliving the attack. But what's strange is that sometimes the dreams aren't of my attack, but of the attack that I've been told about by the rape victims whom I've been interviewing."

"I'm guessing these dreams are pretty vivid and gruesome?"

"Yes. Some have been really bad. If it weren't for Diego being there, I don't know how I'd cope."

"Are they getting worse or better?"

"Actually, I think they are less severe than they were."

"You know that dreams can sometimes be a natural release of pent up energy or worry?"

"I've heard that."

"Well, it's true. Dreams can accompany any traumatic event. I remember when I had my first miscarriage. I was very young. I had nightmares for quite a while, but in time they went away. I stayed busy and my next pregnancy went very well. Time can really heal all wounds. People say that, but it really is true. You don't ever forget bad things that happen to

The Urge

you, but the sadness and grief go away. I'm sure that in time your nightmares over this attack will leave you. I'm sure you have lots of work at the station and with your art to keep your mind busy. Also, having Diego there with you will help. And you can always call me up or come over and talk. I'm always here for you too."

"Thank you," said Marielena. "And how are you doing?"

"I'm fine. I can't seem to find enough hours to clean, cook, go to mass, and see my friends and family."

The conversation continued until Diego came walking in, acting surprised to see their dear friend, Señora Santiago. He had bought enough food to feed the Señora as well as the two of them. They sat down to all the carryout and the flan. It was much, much later, after Señora Santiago had gone home that Marielena said, "Did you think you were going to feed an army that you brought all that carryout home? Or did you know that Señora Santiago would be here?"

Diego laughed and said, "You're too smart for your own good, you know. Yes, I planned to have her come talk to you. I thought it would do you good."

"My dear husband, you always know me so well. Yes, it did help. She is such a kind and caring person who always knows what to say to me. It was so relaxing to sit and visit with her. Between your love and hers, I think that was exactly what I needed tonight."

And it was. There were no more nightmares, not that night, nor any others.

~ ~

Chapter 17
Back Home

Marielena's arm healed nicely, but slowly. She returned to work immediately and added her own name, the location of the attack, and her observations of the serial rapist to her charts. There were two parts of the attack that made no sense to her. First, she, like the other women who had seen his face, had seen him somewhere before. She ought to be able to name her assailant. Second, she knew that she had slashed her attacker's face with her car keys, but he hadn't uttered a sound when the keys went down the left side of his face from his eye to his chin. All he had done was get angry and slam her into the street signpost. The result was her broken arm. He had wisely chosen a part of the street where there was no streetlight so he could lay in wait for her and where she would have a hard time recognizing him. But even so, she had thought he looked familiar.

Her attack description was in the newspapers, and she received notes and letters from Professor Villars and the students. Several of the students expressed

The Urge

remorse that they hadn't accompanied her to her hotel when she left the bar. Professor Villars stated again how sorry he was about not being able to stay for the rest of the party and not seeing her to her hotel. He reiterated he was sorry that he had made other plans for the evening before the students had suggested the party for her. She responded back to all of the notes and letters telling them that there was no way they could have foreseen that she would become the target of the serial rapist that evening. It was simply unfortunate. She again thanked Professor Villars for inviting her to speak with his students and told him how much she had enjoyed the experience.

Sitting in her office and going over all the files, she had a gut feeling that there were some pieces of the puzzle that were eluding her. But what were they?

Two weeks passed and, finally, another attack was reported. This time a young- woman in the heart of the main business district of Madrid had been raped. She had worked overtime in a financial office and was on her way home in the dark. While she hadn't been physically hurt, other than the rape, she was extremely, emotionally upset, as her boyfriend had warned her about working so late when there was a rapist on the loose. She agonized, not only over the fact that she had been raped, but also that her boyfriend might not want "damaged goods". She expressed her concerns when Marielena interviewed her. The girl said she hadn't even thought of the consequences of the rape until two days afterward when her boyfriend acted "cold" toward her and kept saying, "I told you so." Marielena sympathized with her and said, "If your boyfriend really loves you, he may come around. He's probably as mad at himself for not coming to escort you home as he is at you. After all, it isn't your fault this crazy person is out there. Keep in mind that I too

Chapter 17

could have been one of his victims."

As she spoke to this girl, she realized that it had to be the same rapist. The M.O. was the same, as well as the girl's fragmented description of him. He was tall, soft-spoken, and extremely strong, and he had knocked her out to escape. The girl even stated that the rapist had looked somewhat familiar. When Marielena showed the girl her sketch of the rapist, the girl identified him. It was the same man.

Evidently, this rapist had all his moves down to some sort of a format. Almost as if he were repeating the same actions over and over again. Perhaps, as he would if he were in a play or stage performance. He was creating the same scene again and again. He was the main actor, but his leading lady changed. The results, however, were the same. He was satisfied sexually for the moment, but he had to repeat the scene to continue to be sexually, psychologically, and/or physiologically satiated. Somehow it didn't seem to be a coincidence that his actions were always choreographed in the same way. She wrote three questions on the margin of her main chart:

Could the rapist have had theatrical experience? Was he an actor?

Could the rapist have ever been identified as having criminally or sexually/ deviate behaviors or tendencies and have received psychiatric help somewhere?

Since the list of rapes in and around the Madrid area had occurred roughly over a three-year period, had the rapist just moved to the Madrid area during the last three years? If so, could his prior rapes, if there were any, with the same M.O. have occurred somewhere else before those three years? Where? She wrote in red, "Check newspapers of other Spanish cities prior to these three years."

The Urge

Marielena thought for a while, then she went into her husband's office and shared her ideas. He suggested that she should go to the library and have Señora Antonia Oso, the librarian, help her locate any reports of rapes. He reminded her that Señora Oso had helped Margarita go through past issues of newspapers and periodicals when she was researching her husband's infidelities. Perhaps some of the answers to Marielena's questions were awaiting her in the library.

Marielena went to see Señora Oso the very next day and the following days as well. In a newspaper from Barcelona four years before her existing chart of rapes occurring in the Madrid area, there were a series of rapes around Barcelona. She returned to her office at the police station and called the Barcelona police. Yes, they had searched for a serial rapist at the time of the newspaper articles which she had found, but the rapes had mysteriously stopped. The cases were left in their backlog of unsolved "cold cases". She asked if they had the reports from each of the victims, then who in their department had worked the cases and was that person still in their police force. She wondered if any information they had might still be available to her. Fortunately, the detective who had worked the cases was still on their force and they directed her to him. In fact, to be helpful, they transferred her call directly to him.

Several hours later she had what she needed to confirm the rapes in Barcelona had exactly the same MO, victim descriptions of the rapist's body build, and times of attacks. The Barcelona detective had concluded when the rapes stopped that their rapist had migrated somewhere else. But the detective couldn't answer the questions of who he was or why he had chosen Madrid as his next city for raping victims. What was he doing when he wasn't raping victims? And,

Chapter 17

where had he been before Barcelona?

Again, Marielena returned to the library. She was now looking for any newspaper articles describing a series of rapes anywhere in Spain that had occurred in the last ten years. After searching for two hours, she found a newspaper from the Basque region where again the rapes had mysteriously started and stopped during the course of five years.

Marielena concluded that whoever the rapist was, he must be educated enough to be able to find employment in major cosmopolitan cities from which he could fan out and commit his crimes. But what was this person educated in, what field, what endeavor? That was the real mystery. That information might even give her a clue as to how he sought out his victims.

She decided to approach the search from another angle - that of a person with the theatrical experience. She got on the internet and concluded that every city center from which the rapist had operated was also a cultural center with live theater - sometimes professional and sometimes amateur. But which? And - how could she figure out which? She went home to muse on the subject.

After dinner that evening, she and Diego decided to watch a documentary television. There was a program concerning the exhumation and moving of Francisco Franco's remains from the Valley of the Fallen Mausoleum outside Madrid to the Cemeterio Municipal El Pardo Mingorrubio in Madrid so that his remains would rest beside his wife's. Since it was a documentary, the program was two hours long and included official movie footage and photos of Franco's politics, his friendships with Benito Mussolini and Adolf Hitler, and his dictatorship, from his rise to power in 1939 until his death in 1975. As they watched the

The Urge

documentary, Marielena suddenly reached out and squeezed Diego's arm.

"That's him," she yelled.

"Yes, that's Franco," said Diego.

"No, that's not what I meant," Marielena said. "That's who the serial rapist looks like." She ran to her sketchbook and brought it back. They compared her sketch to pictures of Francisco Franco on the television screen.

"Sure enough," replied Diego. "But how? Why Franco?"

"What if he was wearing a mask of Francisco Franco? That would explain why when I reached out and scratched his face with my keys, he didn't react in any way. I must have cut the mask with my keys. And - that's why he looked familiar to most of his victims. He looked familiar, but we couldn't put a name to the face because it was the face of a dead man. We'd seen the face in our Spanish history books, but with Franco long gone, we couldn't associate the face of a living rapist with him. Wow!"

"Well, that discovery gives you another lead to follow in approaching the problem. You might search costume and theatrical companies for someone who purchased a mask of Franco. Or, you might see if any of the theaters in the cities, where you have reports of a serial rapist being active, ever had a production about Franco. Or maybe had an actor who needed to look like Franco for some reason."

"Great ideas! I'll get on it tomorrow. I don't know why I didn't think of a mask or a disguise before. But another thought just occurred to me, the victim of the most recent rape in Madrid looked at my sketch and said it was the same attacker. If I tore the mask he was

Chapter 17

wearing when he attacked me, did he already have a replacement or did he have to purchase a new one before going out hunting again?"

"Interesting question," Diego replied.

~ ~

Chapter 18
The Search

Where to start? Marielena asked herself this question when she entered her office the next morning. She obtained two huge pieces of paper and tacked them on the wall beside her other charts. One was headed "MASKS" and the other was headed "THEATER PRODUCTIONS." She then added subtitles to each paper. Under "MASKS," she wrote Costume Shops and Theatrical Manufacturers. Under "THEATER PRODUCTIONS," she wrote Amateur versus Professional. As she stared at the headings and tried to decide how to get started, she thought she should begin with the earliest known rape cases that she had found to date - Basque country.

She called the Bilbao police force, identified herself, and then explained her ongoing investigation of rapes that had occurred all over Spain. She said that since the earliest known cases that she had found had taken place in the Basque country, she was calling to speak to the officer who had worked them. Could she please speak to whoever had handled the series

The Urge

of rape cases that she had found in her newspaper search? Unfortunately, the officer in charge of those cases, which were in their cold case files, had retired. His case notes could be emailed to her and the officer, a Señor Etxarrin, could be found living in Arrigorriaga. The officer in charge gave her the telephone number of Señor Etxarrin so that she could speak with him directly.

When she called him, after going over all his faxed notes, she discovered that he, like many retired police officers, had always been haunted by his serial rapist cold cases. He was eager to speak with her and they compared notes. Everything checked out. When she described her attack and her thoughts about the rapist wearing a Franco mask, Señor Etxarrin exclaimed, "You know we had a theater production in the small village, Gernika, around the time of our rapes, and one of the actors wore a mask to play the role of Franco in the play. It made him look exactly like Franco. I'll look to see if I can find anyone who might know anything about the play and the actor."

Marielena said, "That would be wonderful. Maybe my search won't be as difficult as I thought it might be."

A day later Señor Etxarrin called her back and said, "I'm afraid to say I can't give you the name of the actor. When I went to the theater in Gernika, the production manager said there had been a fire and all their contact files of actors were consumed in that fire. Everything in the entire theater was gone, burnt to askes. Their current theater had been built upon the foundation of the old theater. He, himself, had been a young actor at that time and he vaguely remembered the man who played Franco. He described him as a tall, thin, and muscular man who was soft-spoken, polite, and well-educated. He was sort of withdrawn - not anti-

Chapter 18

social, but just sort of aloof from the rest of the cast. He really didn't converse with the other actors and actresses." Señor Etxarrin was sorry that he couldn't give a name to Marielena. "The production manager said that this actor had the main part in that particular production in question, but only bit parts in several other productions during a period of approximately four or five years. Then, the man never showed up again. The manager assumed he had moved and was no longer interested or available to be an actor with them."

"Oh wait," he added. "The production manager thought the actor who played Franco was about 20 or so years old at the time because he himself was about five years younger than the particular actor in question. If that's any help, at least you can estimate his current age."

Marielena was stymied. She had been so sure she was on the right track. On a chart that she put on her office wall, she started making a timeline of the rapist's activities. Even though she knew she was making some wild assumptions, she wrote down the following"

> If he was active here in the Madrid area for 5 years and
> He had moved from Barcelona 4 years before that
> $\qquad$ = 9 years
> Then, if he were active in Barcelona for approximately 4 to 5 years $\qquad$ = 14 years
> And, he had moved to Barcelona from Basque area 5 years before $\qquad$ = 19 years
> And, he had been active in the Basque country for over 5 years $\qquad$ = 24? years
> He started using a Franco mask in the Basque country after the play.

The Urge

Then, she postulated that there were some definite questions which could be answered whenever she put the pieces of the puzzle together. She wrote these on a separate chart in anticipation of needed answers. She would later check off each item as she affirmed the answers. The list she wrote was this:

Where was the rapist before the Basque country?
How long had he been in that area?
What age did he begin raping women?
How old is the rapist now?
Does he have a formal education?
If so, where did he get his degree or degrees?
What was his field of studies?
What is his occupation?
Was he educated in the Basque area 24? years ago - or somewhere else?
Are there records of other rapes before the Basque region?
If so, do they have the same MO? (Over 24 yrs. ago)

Good Grief, she thought. He's been at work for almost a quarter of a century or even longer. Why hasn't someone caught him by now?

She taped a map of Spain on her wall and with a red magic marker, she put X's on the cities where the rapist had been active and then numbered red dotted lines between the cities in chronological order as had been revealed by her research. She asked herself the question - is there a pattern here? What am I missing?

As she continued to look at the map, she realized that the largest city in the Basque region was Bilbao. That fact posed another question. Did the rapist come to the Basque region and Bilbao from the left or from the right, west or east? Also, how old was he when he reached the Bilbao area?

Chapter 18

As she stood looking at the map, Diego came into her office. He said, "You've really been working hard at this. What have you discovered so far?"

"Dead ends," she answered. "It seems our rapist has been at work at least twenty-four or so years. I've traced him back to the Basque region, but now I don't know if he moved there from the east or the west. There were a number of rapes around Bilbao. The detective who worked the cases has discovered there was an actor who wore a Franco mask in a production in Gernika. At that time, the actor was approximately 20 years old, but he couldn't give me a name or better description than the one we already have. All artist contact information files were burned in a fire which occurred at the theater shortly after the time the rapist was an actor there."

"So now what?"

"Well - maybe I need to work east and west to see where he was prior to Bilbao. It would have been over 24 or 25 years ago. Who knows whether I can find anything after so many years?"

Diego said, "Right now I really haven't any other cases which I need to work on, so I could help you if you'd like. Maybe with both of us working, we can be more effective."

"That would be great! I was beginning to feel overwhelmed. Any help you can lend will speed up the search."

"Where were you going to search?"

"It seems the rapist specializes in larger metropolitan areas. To the west of Bilboa is Santander, Oviedo, and Gijon. I was going to work on those areas first. To the east of San Sebastian in Spain, there's Toulouse in France. The other towns are much smaller. To the

The Urge

southeast of San Sebastian is Pamplona. I seriously doubt that our rapist would want to be in any really small town unless it were a suburb of a larger city where he feels safe and thrives. It doesn't seem to fit the list of rapes that I've compiled. She gestured to the charts and the map on her office wall. Also, if he went far enough southeast of Pamplona, he'd be back in Barcelona."

"I doubt he'd rape victims going back toward an area which he'd left months or years before since his M.O. doesn't seem to change," said Diego.

"What if I contact the police in San Sebastian and Pamplona, and you contact the police in Santander, Oviedo, and Gijon?" Asked Marielena. "If we don't find anything in any of those places, I'll contact Toulouse across the border in France," said Marielena. "Who knows, our rapist might originally be French."

"Maybe we'll get lucky and find a record of rapes with the same M.O. prior to Bilbao."

"It will be so nice to have you helping me," said Marielena. "Oh, you might also ask about anyone, having the same description, being in any kind of theater production in those cities. Remember that at that time period, the rapist would have had to have been around twenty years or younger."

~ ~

Chapter 19
Retired Police Officer Etxarrin

Tonyo Etxarrin sat in his apartment in Arrigorriaga looking out his living room window. He watched the river flowing along beside his building and wondered how often he had sat there thinking when he was still on the police force. During those sitting sessions, he had felt himself trying to get into the minds of the criminals whom he was trying to catch. In his thirty years on the force, he had discovered that sometimes you had to put yourself in your quarry's shoes to be able to make an arrest. People were always people. Humans were humans. People, regardless of how smart they were or how smart they thought they were, always made mistakes - human mistakes. No one is infallible. Sometimes the mistakes were so glaringly obvious and quickly discovered that you laughed as you came upon the preposterous blunder. You were still laughing as you slapped the cuffs on the offender and hauled him or her away to jail. At times though, the mistake or mistakes would remain hidden for a long time, sometimes years. Police departments always

The Urge

had files of cold cases. Many of these files were locked away for decades before one small clue, which had previously been overlooked, jumped out, like a snake hiding in the grass. At times it was a series of little things, which when added to newly discovered facts, completed the big picture so that an arrest could be made - a perp who had thought he would never be caught could be put behind bars. And - sometimes, it took new eyes and new information to point one in the right direction to finish the case.

He had been pleasantly surprised by the call from Detective Marielena Cortez-Rivera. If what she had described to him were true, her new eyes and new information would finally put to rest several cases from the Bilbao Police Department cold-case rape files.

He went to his file cabinet and took out several of his personal notebooks which he had kept on those cold cases. He took the notebooks back to his living room chair and stacked them on the end table. Then we went into the kitchen and poured ourselves another cup of coffee from the coffee pot. He took his cup and added it to the end table. This might be an interesting morning reading through his notebooks.

Slowly he reread his old notes. One case concerned a schoolteacher who had worked late and was raped in the school parking lot as she left school for home. He noticed she had reported seeing her rapist's face, and thought he looked familiar, but couldn't identify him. She had been knocked out. When she awoke, she was lying in the same spot where she'd been attacked. He looked for any physical description of her and found she had been petite. She described her attacker as a much stronger individual than she. She hadn't fought because she felt she wouldn't be able to overpower him anyway. Yes, this rape sounded like the same M.O. that Detective Cortez-Rivera had described.

Chapter 19

He moved on to a second case which had been committed three months after the first case. Here, a young woman had taken a train from Bilbao to visit her mother in the neighboring town of Basauri. Returning from Basauri, she arrived at the Bilbao train station around midnight. When he left the train station to walk home, he was attacked and raped. The raped had occurred only two blocks from her home in a dark alley. His notes stated she had reported feeling like she had been followed; but every time she had looked behind her, she had seen no one. She evidently should have followed her instincts. She was attacked from behind by a man who she described as slim and muscular. He had recorded that she, also, was a small woman. She hadn't seen her attacker, but she had been knocked out and found herself lying in the alley.

As he continued to read case after case that morning, he realized seven of the nine cases he had recorded in his personal notebooks were very similar to Detective Cortez-Rivera's cases. They spanned a time period of four years. After that time period, the same M.O. cases ceased. The last two cases in his personal notebook had a complete MO. He remembered himself wondering during those years and remembered he had assumed the rapist had changed his MO. Now he concluded that the early assumption was a false one. The last two rapes had to have been committed by someone entirely different.

He knew the Bilbao department had arrested a couple of rapists, but they hadn't followed either of the Mos of the earlier cases. One had raped an ex-girlfriend who was now dating someone else, and one had raped a child. The first had been a rape of passion, and the second a rape committed by a pedophile.

The seven rapes fit the M.O. he had discussed with Detective Cortez-Rivera. She had received a faxed,

The Urge

official department set of notes which had been filed years ago before she had called him. Their discussion had gone over those official notes. What was interesting to him, as he perused his personal notes, was how his official departmental notes were backed up by his personal notes from his notebooks. He congratulated himself. He really had been a good cop. He just hadn't had all the information that she had available now.

Thinking back, he remembered how he had carried such a huge workload during those years. The department hadn't been as large as it was even when he retired. He hadn't been able to sit and think for hours. Even if he had the luxury of those thinking hours, the lack of information had plagued him. He had always wondered what he could have done to help solve these cases. When the rapes had ended, he'd been almost relieved – but these cases never seemed to leave his mind entirely. Periodically, he had called his buddies in the department; but no, they hadn't solved these cases. They were still in the cold files.

Putting away his notebooks and taking his last sip of, by then, cold coffee, he made up his mind to ask everyone he knew, both at the department and personally, if they could remember the play in Gernika or anything about the actor who played Franco. He would do everything he could to help Detective Cortez-Rivera. It would be both a professional and personal victory to be of assistance in putting away this rapist.

~ ~

Chapter 20
Diego Helps Marielena

Diego went to his office and called the police office in Santander, the largest of the cities west of Bilbao. After identifying himself to the officer in charge, he described the cases that he was currently working on. He stated how he and one of his detectives were tracking a serial rapist, who seemed to always follow the same M.O. in his rapes. Diego stated that his office had been able to trace the perp backward from Madrid to Barcelona, and then to the Basque region around Bilbao.

So far, their records extended back at least twenty-four years to the time the rapist was somewhere between twenty and twenty-five years old. He then explained that one of their sources had linked the rapist to a possible actor who had played Francisco Franco in a production in Gernika. He continued his narration by saying that all victims had described the rapist as being tall and muscular, but thin, polite, and soft-spoken. He asked if their department had on record any cases active or archived that involved a suspect or conviction of anyone fitting this description in the last twenty-five years.

The officer assured Diego that he would check their records as soon as he had a spare moment and get back to him with any pertinent information. Since he was extremely busy, it might take a few days.

Diego thanked him and continued his search westward by calling the Oviedo and Gijón police departments. He received the same responses from both of them.

While he was waiting for any answers, he went into Marielena's office and asked, "What other leads can I check on?"

She answered, "Remember to call various theaters, both professional and amateur, in the cities in question and see if they had any actors who matched our rapist's physical characteristics. I know it's a long shot, but we might get lucky."

"Good idea," said Diego as he returned to his office and Googled theaters and theatrical groups both professional and amateur for each city.

Meanwhile, Marielena started calling police stations in San Sebastian, Pamplona, and Toulouse. As with Diego, all the police stations said they had no active rape cases on file, but they would check out their cold cases and get back to her. It would probably take a while.

Several days later, Diego got news back from Oviedo and Gijón. They both came up empty-handed. They had no active or archived cases that matched. Dead end!

Marielena, however, had better news. While she received negative responses from Pamplona and

Chapter 20

Toulouse police departments, she got a hit from the San Sabastian station. They reported that approximately twenty-eight years ago there had been a series of three rapes that had taken place over the period of four years. The description given by all three victims matched the description of the suspect currently sought by police in connection with the most recent attacks - tall, slender, muscular, soft-spoken, and polite.

They also reported in a nearby town called Irun, close to the Spanish cities of Pamplona and the city of Biarritz, there had been a reported rape of a very young girl who had ended up pregnant. She had reported that a young teenage boy had raped her in a playground. She didn't know the boy, had never seen him before, and never saw him again later. She had described him as being tall, slender, muscular, soft-spoken, polite, gentle, and almost loving. At the time of her rape, she had been distraught over an argument with her boyfriend. The rapist, who seemed to appear out of nowhere, began speaking to her with compassion for her plight using kind words of reassurance. She had said he shared with her that he too was unloved and unwanted. After their discussion, he had taken advantage of her and the situation. The result was she had conceived a child.

The detective said that he'd tried to track down the now full-grown woman but had no success. He did have her name and would continue his search. It might be a few days before he had any results. Also, he would try to find out the name of her child.

Marielena asked, "So if you couldn't find the mother, you also couldn't find the child. Is that correct?"

"Yes", he answered, "I'm sorry that I can't supply more information at this time."

The Urge

She then asked him, "Do you know of any theatrical productions that took place around the same time frame as the rapes? Specifically, productions with the participation of a teenage actor that fit the description given of the rapist. Are there any professional theaters in Irun?"

"No there are no professional theaters there. It is such a small town. But, yes. I believe there were some amateur productions at the local middle and high school around that same time, but it was such a long time ago, I doubt anyone would have any record of them. I'll look to see if anyone here at the station can remember anything about them. We do have a few older men in the community who were on the force around that time. I'll ask."

Marielena thanked him for his time and information. She then went to her chart of rapes and added to the list:

```
Approx. Age.
15 to 16   Irun    teen/ possibly first rape/ school play?
16 to 19   San Sebastian      high school/ three rapes
20 to 25   Bilbao actor Gernika/college/ more rapes
26 to 31   Barcelona          job?  What? / more rapes
32 to 40   Madrid             job?  What? / more rapes
```

She stopped to think for a moment and asked herself, have I recorded all the rapes and calculated the ages that they were committed correctly? If so, she knew the rapist currently had to be in his forties. That would mean he is currently in his prime both as a rapist and as some sort of professional.

She continued to wonder:

If the rapist went to college, it would have to have been during his years in the Basque region.

Chapter 20

But what was his major?

What college did he attend? He must have acquired a degree that had allowed him to have a successful career, one which had afforded him the possibility of transferring his professional activity to multiple cities. The fact of the matter is it's much easier for an educated person to find employment opportunities that provide that kind of mobility. It is not so easy in Spain for someone who is uneducated. An uneducated person in Spain usually stays in one area, and it's usually the area where they were born. They may have some sort of occupation, but not a high-paying one nor one that allows for high mobility.

Marielena decided to follow her own advice to Diego and started researching the live theaters in San Sebastian. After several calls, she located a theater that had been in business for thirty years and hired people of all ages. Unfortunately, the person with whom she spoke had only been employed there for three years and had no knowledge of prior productions or cast members. Again, dead-end!

As she entered Diego's office, he got a call from the Santander police office to say that after looking through all their cold case files, there had been none that matched Diego's rapist, either by description or MO. Diego looked up at Marielena and said, "that was another dead end. I also had no success in finding theaters with any actor matching our rapist's description, but at least we know the rapist didn't start west of Bilbao. Have you had any luck?"

Marielena sat down in the chair opposite him and said, "Yes, somewhat. San Sabastian police told me of several rapes matching our rapist and his MO. One was from a small town called Irun where the girl ended up pregnant."

The Urge

"Really?"

"Yes, but they can't find her. She must be in her forties now and has probably moved away, and/or maybe married. She could have even changed her name. Another dead end, but they promised to continue looking for her," she concluded with a sigh. "I've made a chart of dates, places, and possible ages of the rapist. If he were a teenager in the area of Biarritz and committed rape in Irun, he could have been in high school in San Sabastian and in college in the Basque region. What was his major and what degree did he get there? I'd really like to know."

"Well - it seems we're getting closer," replied Diego. "Have you searched out what colleges are in that area?"

"No, not yet. I keep thinking I'm missing something; but whatever it is, it keeps eluding me."

"At least we know his age and one of his interests - theater. Maybe he's interested in something related to the theater? Maybe languages? Maybe literature? Maybe music? Maybe art? What else would be like theatre?" Asked Diego. "And, what school or schools, Bilbao or in the Basque region, would specialize in those things?"

"OK, that sends me in a new direction," said Marielena.

At that point in the conversation, Deputy Ortega came into the commissioner's office. As he entered, he said, "I'm glad you're both here. Another rape has been reported in the town of Mastoles, just south of Madrid. Detective José Martinez said that the victim wants to talk to Detective Marielena Cortez-Rivera about the rape as soon as possible.

Marielena replied, "I'll call José immediately and

Chapter 20

make arrangements to do so immediately."

She left Diego's office for her own and called, making plans to go to Madrid the very next day to speak with the victim, Maria Alvelar Clarita Casas Jerez. While speaking to José Martinez, the detective, she received the good news that Maria, who had contacted the police immediately upon being raped, hadn't cleaned herself up prior to the official medical examination. Pubic hair, not hers but the rapist's, had been found. The rapist was finally getting sloppy and had left behind a DNA sample. Marielena hoped it would match the DNA sample taken from the fingernails of their other victim from Seville. Maybe at last they would be able to catch the rapist.

~~

Chapter 21
Marielena
Returns to Madrid

In the Madrid police station, Maria Alvelar sat across the desk from Marielena and looked at her expectantly as though Marielena could do something immediately to help her. Maria was a young woman almost exactly the same size as Marielena. She had a dark purple bruise on her jaw where the rapist had hit her to make his escape.

Marielena asked her quietly, "I understand you were raped the day before yesterday?"

"Yes," replied Maria. "I had gone shopping with my best friend in the late afternoon. Then we went out to dinner, to a tapas bar, and dancing. Her boyfriend met us at the bar and went dancing with us. After midnight they went home and since I was only three blocks from my apartment, I went home alone. Big mistake! I've known about a serial rapist in the Madrid area, I've read all the newspaper reports, I've seen the television broadcasts; but, somehow, I didn't believe it could happen to me. I was such a fool!"

The Urge

"Don't be too hard on yourself," said Marielena. "I was almost a victim myself, and I was already working on the case trying to find him. I knew all about him. I found myself in the wrong place at the wrong time."

"Really?" asked Maria.

"Yes. Now tell me all your story just as you remember it."

"Well - I walked past an underground parking garage and a hand reached out and grabbed me. The man said, 'do as I tell you, don't scream, and I won't hurt you'."

"And?"

"And then he stuffed something in my mouth, held my arms behind my back, and dragged me further down into the parking garage."

"What did he sound like?"

"That was what was funny because he was very soft-spoken, polite, almost apologetic. His voice wasn't very deep. He almost seemed comforting."

"Do you remember what he did then?"

"He pushed me down, tore at my slacks and panties, and then forced himself on me. I was terrified."

"Did you get a look at his face?"

"Yes, and I almost thought that I knew him. He looked so familiar."

"Can you describe him?"

"He had a receding hairline, small brown mustache, and brownish-colored hair."

"And his eyes?" asked Marielena.

"His eyes seemed to be really deep-set, and almost

Chapter 21

too small for his face - it was as if he didn't have eyes. Strange looking."

Marielena got out her sketch of the serial rapist and a photograph that she had copied of Franco and turned them both face-down on the desk. Turning over only her sketch, she asked, "Does this look like your attacker?"

Maria answered, "Yes, almost. It still isn't exactly like him. Is this a sketch that was made from descriptions of other victims?"

"Yes," replied Marielena. "Now I want you to look at a copied photograph and tell me if it is a photograph of your rapist?"

As she turned over the photograph of Franco, Maria gasped and said, "That's him! Who is he?"

Marielena answered, "We don't know yet, but we believe we're getting closer to finding him. Please don't share this information with anyone."

"No, I won't; but I'm so glad you're going to catch him. I can't stop reliving his attack on me. I'll never feel completely safe until I know he's behind bars."

Marielena thanked Maria for her cooperation and allowed her to leave the interrogation room. Marielena sat back in her chair and mused, the mask - that's the key. He must have gotten another one, since every victim that reported rapes after the failed attempt on my person, has positively identified Franco as the rapist. I think my next step is to find where one can obtain a Franco mask. If anyone has recently purchased a replacement mask for the one which I ruined, I'll know who our rapist is. I don't know why I didn't follow this path before now. I feel I've wasted a lot of time.

The Urge

As she thought some more she said, "maybe not though. What I've done so far is trace his whole life of crime, build a strong case against him, and compile a list of victims. I've also figured out his age, that he's educated, that he likes the theater and acting, and that he's been able to move and change jobs. We also have two samples of his DNA, one from Seville and one from Madrid, fingernail deposits of skin, and pubic hair. When we do find him, we'll have a solid case against him, and we'll be able to put him away for a long time. No, the time hasn't been wasted at all. Now I need to go back to my office in San Anton and add Maria's information to my charts. Before I do that, while I'm in Madrid maybe I should check out the costume and theatrical supply companies for Franco masks. If he is currently working in the Madrid area and raping women here and is doing so with a new Franco mask, maybe he got it in this area."

She was about to get up and leave when Detective Martinez came in and asked, "Was the session with Maria Alvelar productive?"

"Yes, I was able to confirm that her attacker is the same rapist we've been trying to find. I think he is wearing a mask during his attacks. Please do not release that information to any reporters, because I think the mask is a significant lead. I don't want that information to reach the rapist, or he may move on or change his M.O. before we can catch him. Now - where in Madrid would one buy a mask?"

Marielena and José sat together at one of the station's computers and googled costume shops and theatrical supply houses in the Madrid area. It was amazing that in a city of almost three-and-a-quarter million people and a metropolitan area of over six-and-a-half million square kilometers, there were only thirty costume shops and four large theatrical supply

Chapter 21

houses. Regardless, Marielena and José made a list of the establishments and estimated it would take Marielena several days to contact them all either in person or on the phone.

They also searched the Internet for Franco masks. It seemed that only Amazon had sold them; however, Amazon had discontinued selling these particular masks several months prior. It looked like they had not been a big seller. Marielena felt discouraged because it seemed she was just starting to chase this lead looking for a Franco mask; but also felt encouraged since she realized the purchase of the mask by the rapist was so recent that he couldn't have gotten it on Amazon. A purchase from Amazon would have made tracing the sale a real nightmare.

José apologized that he didn't have the time to help her. Marielena was on her own. She left the station with a map of the city with each establishment marked. Two of the costume stores were within walking distance from the station so she checked those out before going home to San Anton. Neither of the stores had Franco masks nor had they ever had them. She marked them off her list.

Reaching her office much later she added Maria's information to her charts and checked in with Diego. She updated him on her list of costume and theatrical supply establishments and told him she'd already checked out two costume stores with no success.

As they were speaking Marielena received a phone call from Police Commissioner Jorge Badaztain in San Sebastian. He said that one of his police officers had told him about Marielena's search for a rapist in their area and about a specific rape that occurred years ago in Irun. While he couldn't say who the rapist was, he did have the name of the woman, really a

The Urge

girl at the time of the rape. He also had the name of the child whom the rapist had fathered. The woman's name was Helena Diez Urbi de Leon Silva. She was currently living in the town of Getaria with a sister. She had never married. The child's name was Henri Diez Urbi de Leon Silva, and he was living in San Sebastian and working in a restaurant as a chef.

Marielena asked, "Could I possibly speak to both the mother and the son?"

The Commissioner said, "Yes, to both. I personally know the son. He is one of my neighbors and I'm sure he could arrange for you to speak with his mother. Of course, you would have to come to San Sebastian, but we could set up your interview with them both here at the station. I doubt either he or his mother would be able to come to Toledo or Madrid. I'm not sure either travel much. She is in her late forties, and he is in his early thirties, but he works full-time. She has been crippled with arthritis and tendonitis for years. He could bring her to San Sebastian, so you could interview them both on the same day."

"That would be great," replied Marielena. "Is it possible you could set up a date and time and let me know? I'll gladly clear my calendar and come to speak with them."

Commissioner Badaztain said, "Of course. I'll contact them, make arrangements, and let you know. Is there any day or time that is inconvenient?"

"No," she replied. "I'll come whenever you arrange the meeting. My commissioner will let me come anytime."

~ ~

Chapter 22
Marielena Travels to San Sebastian

Marielena had never been to the northern part of Spain. She was amazed at how green the landscape was. So many trees, and the mountains seemed to go on and on forever. When she reached San Sebastian, she realized it was no wonder the Spanish monarchs had loved being there. La Concha, the beach, and the old town were beautiful with the Iglesia de Santa Maria, the quaint buildings, and the view of the high peninsula jutting outward with the statue of Christ. The fishing port and the smells of the sea beckoned to her, but she walked to the police station as soon as she could break free from all the wondrous sites which assailed her in this absolutely beautiful city. She was happy she had arranged to arrive two hours early for her appointment.

She entered the station and asked for Police Commissioner Jorge Badaztain, she hoped she had pronounced his name correctly. Basque words were so different from Spanish words. She was escorted into a small office on the second floor where she had a

The Urge

formal introduction to the commissioner. She asked where Helena and Henri were, and the Commissioner stated they were waiting in a small reception room. He said that he wanted to speak to her prior to their meeting.

He said, "I told both Henri and Helena what you have been working on. They are both anxious to tell you what they know. Unfortunately, I'm afraid it is very little."

"I'm sorry to hear that," replied Marielena.

"What I've thought about, they may not be ready for, but I wanted to ask you first about it, unbeknownst to them before you meet."

"What is that?" Asked Marielena.

"Have you considered taking a DNA sample from both of them?"

"The thought had crossed my mind," said Marielena.

"If you got a DNA sample from them, you could have the DNA of Henri compared to a suspected rapist. It would prove the rapist is his father and it would also be proof of his crime against Helena. Even though it was years ago, it would give you even more evidence to convict the rapist."

"Yes, it would, but do you think they would be willing to submit to DNA tests?"

"They realize the stigma of having a child out of wedlock has always affected both their lives. Henri has always been angry that his mother was so mistreated. They've waited for years to get some sort of closure to their situation. Henri was made fun of as a child and both he and his mother were subjected to verbal abuse by neighbors. You know how petty small-town people can be, how vicious. The abuse was why they

Chapter 22

moved away from Irun and went to live in Getaria. Henri grew up there telling everyone that his father had died. Later, he came to San Sebastian, went to chef school, and became a chef in one of our leading restaurants. But the pain was still there, just hidden behind a facade of bravado. I think they might be willing to give samples of saliva for DNA matching. I just didn't want to suggest it for the first time in front of them."

"I understand. I also think it's a good idea. It definitely would help my case against the rapist - if we are ever able to find him."

"OK. I'll stay with you as you question them if you like, and we'll wait until what we feel is the appropriate time to make the suggestion about DNA samples and testing."

"Sounds like a good plan," said Marielena.

With that decided, they stood, and Commissioner Badaztain opened the door leading from his office into the small reception room next door.

Introductions were made and, as Marielena looked at Helena, she realized that they were both about the same size, coloring, and weight. The only difference was that Helena was older. Again, Marielena was struck by the similarities of all the rapist's victims. The rapist did indeed have a set pattern for his attack and his victims. And - he had been following his diabolical course throughout his entire life. He had to be stopped.

Marielena asked Helena to relive her attack as best as she could. She encouraged her to take her time, as she might not remember every detail since so many years had passed.

Helena took a deep breath and, reaching out and clasping her son's right hand, said, "Yes, it's been a

The Urge

long time, but I remember clearly what happened. I've relived it over and over again, not only when I'm awake, but also in my dreams."

Her son patted his mother's hand with his left hand and said, "Just take your time, Mother."

Helena said, "I was with a number of friends and had just broken up with my boyfriend. I had turned seventeen and I thought my life was over. It's funny how your thinking changes as you age. Looking back, I probably should have been grateful I'd broken up with my boyfriend as he had been verbally abusive with me during our courtship, but I was so sad. I felt alone and unloved. I had a lot to learn at that age. I left my friends and wandered into a playground. At first, I didn't see the boy who was probably a year or two years younger than I. He was sitting on one of the swings. I sat on a bench and was crying. I think he watched me for several minutes before coming over to me. He was so quiet and caring. He asked me gently what my problem was - no, he asked me why I was crying. I didn't answer him at first, so he asked again. As I continued to cry, he put an arm around me and stroked my back - the way one comforts a small child. I continued crying, but finally, I told him that I had just broken up with my boyfriend and I felt very unloved."

"And then?" Asked Marielena.

"He held me close and rocked me back and forth. He said, 'I know all about being unloved and unwanted.' I asked him, 'You do?'"

Helena's son patted his mother and asked, "Are you sure you're up to doing this?"

"Yes," replied Helena. "It's just so hard."

"I know," he answered her.

Chapter 22

Helena took a deep breath and then began again. "He told me, 'Of course, my parents neither love nor want me. Like you, I'm all alone'." Helena stopped for a moment and then added, "We held each other close for a while, and after probably twenty minutes or so, we got up and he walked me over to where the shadows were deeper. I didn't resist him. I'm not sure what I thought he was going to do, but then, he forcibly removed my jeans and panties and raped me."

"Did you scream or fight or do anything to stop him?" Asked Marielena.

"It was as if I were in a trance. I didn't yell, but I did keep saying, 'no, no, no. I couldn't believe I was being raped."

"What did he do after that?"

"He hit me. I must have blacked out because, when I woke up, I was still lying there, and he was gone."

"What did you do then?" Asked Marielena.

"I went home and tried to tell my parents what had happened. My father was very angry and stormed out of the house. My mother tried to comfort me. Later I learned that my dad and one of his friends had gone to the playground, but it was totally deserted. My attacker wasn't there or anywhere else they looked. They walked through our entire village, but there was no one there that they didn't know. A month later we realized I was pregnant because I missed my period. Because the entire family is devout Catholic, I couldn't get an abortion. Our Priest said that I had to keep the baby as God had decided I should be a mother. He didn't even suggest that I go over to one of the nearer towns that had a refuge for unwed mothers. I really don't understand that, but the result of my rape was Henri." She reached over and patted her

The Urge

son's cheek. "He was such a good boy and now he has grown up to be a strong and reliant man as well as a caring and dedicated son. Sadly, we both have suffered humiliation and rejection by our neighbors. And - when it would have been time for me to marry, no one wanted a woman like me with an illegitimate child."

"He ruined your life, Mother," said Henri. "Maybe we can help put him behind bars for life." He looked expectantly at Marielena and the police commissioner.

Marielena asked, "Can you remember what he looked like?"

Helena said, "He was tall, thin, soft-spoken, polite; actually, quite good-looking. As he raped me, I took a good look at him. I'd say he looked a little like Henri, or rather Henri looks like he did. Brown hair, brown eyes, pale-complected. Different coloration than Henri because Henri has my dark complexion with black hair and eyes."

Marielena looked again at Henri and asked, "Could we photograph Henri for comparison if we find the rapist? Also, the commissioner and I have discussed another way you could help. Would you both be willing to give a sample of your DNA so that when we find this man, we can prove he is your father, Henri?"

Henri shook his head and said forcefully, "No, I don't want him as a father, but I would like to see him pay for all the misery which he has caused my mother. I'd like to see him rot in jail for the rest of his life. Of course, we'll give you our DNA samples. Right, Mother?"

Helena said, "Of course we will."

Commissioner Badaztain had already arranged for the saliva DNA tests to be available and a camera, so

Chapter 22

it was only about another half hour before Helena and her son left the station.

Marielena thanked the commissioner, vowed to keep him abreast of the investigation, and, after collecting the DNA samples to take with her, left the station herself. Somehow, she felt she had again missed something, but she couldn't put her finger on what it was.

~ ~

Chapter 23
Back in San Anton

Returning home, Marielena updated Diego on the results of her interview with Helena and Henri. "They were very nice people and they both willingly submitted saliva samples for a DNA match if we ever find this horrible rapist. I left the samples at our police station before I came home. On the way home, however, I had a frightening thought."

"What was that?" Diego asked.

"It seems to me that our rapist is always one step ahead of the police. He moves away from each city before the police can make an identification. Why is he always leaving just about the time the police have enough evidence to prove they are dealing with a serial rapist? He relocates himself into a new city and then starts all over again. How is that?"

"Yes - and?"

"It is as if he has access to police records and knows what the police were doing?"

The Urge

"Hummmmmm."

"What if he were a policeman himself?"

"Oh, I see what you mean. If he checked individual municipalities, then he would be able to see that the local police were building a case for a serial rapist in that location, and how far along they were in their investigation. If Spain had a joint database, he'd only be able to check one source. Unfortunately, the different areas of Spain can't seem to agree to do that. But if he were interested in only one area, the area he was committing rapes in, and checked that one area, he'd know when to move to another city to keep from being discovered."

"Exactly."

"That's an interesting theory."

"The rapist could also keep track of investigations involving rapes in other areas by tapping into their data so he wouldn't move into an area that was already investigating rapes. Also, if he were a policeman, he could fairly easily transfer to a different police station in a different city. Look at how easily you transferred from the Madrid police station to here in San Anton. Good cops are always needed, especially in major metropolitan areas."

"Well, I suppose that could explain how he's moved around from city to city," said Diego skeptically.

Marielena continued then by saying, "If the rapist is a police officer; however, wouldn't I have run across something while researching in all the different stations all over the country? Aren't they smart enough to have asked themselves this same question, whether one of their own officers could possibly be the rapist involved in all their unsolved cases? So far, I've not heard any of them questioning their own officers. All I've gotten

Chapter 23

is that the rapes stopped abruptly; then they surmised that their rapist had moved on. If it were one of their own men, someone somewhere might have linked the cessation of rapes to the leaving of one of their own officers. No one has even made that suggestion to me."

"I know if that circumstance happened here, I would ultimately make that conclusion, even if I thought I knew the officer really well."

"So, we can assume that the rapist isn't a policeman?"

"Probably, but let's not put that idea to rest until we have more information."

"OK. We'll put that on the back burner for now. What else can we assume?"

"While you were out of town, I was thinking and have come up with another angle. I think we need to find someone who just purchased a new Franco mask. We sort of left that issue hanging. Didn't you say the last two recent attacks and rapes were committed by someone who looked like Franco according to the victims?"

"Yes, that's true," said Marielena. "I had started down that path when I was in Madrid and had checked out two costume shops, but the number of places to check out seemed really huge."

"That's OK. I'll help. We aren't really busy right now at the station, so I have some extra time. Give me half the list. We'll divide and conquer."

Marielena said, "That would really help. Also, I think I'll make a sketch of what Henri would look like twenty years from now. Helena stated that Henri looks very much like his father looked when he was younger,

The Urge

except for his coloring. It might cut our work in half to be able to show an image to shopkeepers in theatrical supply houses and costume stores."

"Good thinking," said Diego.

That afternoon, instead of Marielena getting out her sketchbook, Diego and Marielena worked with a graphic artist who specialized in computer enhancement of photographic images. The graphic artist claimed that technology was wonderful in aging a person's image and he could have the images they wanted in a few hours. While it took the photo expert the entire afternoon, he came up with a series of pictures of Henri. Each one showed an older version of Henri in increments of two years. When the resulting images were finally finished, the expert brought in the entire series of images and showed them to Marielena and Diego. He laid the pictures out on Diego's desk. As the last image was shown to them of Henri being approximately forty-five years old. Marielena gasped, "Oh, no! It can't be! It can't be him!"

"Who?" Asked Diego.

"Professor Villars," said Marielena. "Well - that puts to bed the idea that the rapist might be a police officer. I feel bad to have even suggested that possibility. How could I have assumed an officer might be such a monster? At least, now we know who the rapist is."

Diego asked, "Don't beat yourself up over your hunch that the rapist might be a policeman. When you've been working as a policeman for years, as I have, sometimes it pays to have an open mind as to who might be the perp. But Villars -- do all the facts line up?"

Marielena answered, "Yes. He is tall, thin, muscular I think, soft-spoken, and almost compassionate.

Chapter 23

Everything fits. But - how can we prove it? No wonder he disappeared during the night of the party. His 'other plans' that night were to attack and rape me. He must have chosen me as a victim when he saw my pictures in the newspaper about the commission at the city hall. I fit his stereotypic 'perfect victim'. I'm so glad you had me take those self-defense classes with Master Chow."

Turning to the photo expert, she asked, "Is it possible to change this image so that instead of black hair and eyes with a dark complexion, you can make the person have light brown hair, brown eyes, and a pale complexion?"

"Absolutely, let me go make that change and I'll be right back."

Several minutes later he returned with a new image. As he showed it to Marielena, she exclaimed, "Now that really is Professor Villars. It looks just like him. Perfect. I'm so glad we have the whole series of pictures throughout the aging process. They will be very useful as we continue our investigation and begin to put together the case against him. It will be good to go back and again use them in interviewing people. Could you do the entire series with the lighter brown hair, brown eyes, and pale complexion? And, can you make an even younger picture, perhaps as young as approximately fourteen years old? Even though we may not need them since after that first rape, as far as we know, he used a Franco mask."

Within forty-five minutes the photo expert was back with a new series of photos showing Professor Villars from when he was approximately the age during the rape of Helena to Villars's present age.

Marielena thanked him profusely. Turning to Diego she said, "Now it is even more important to find the

The Urge

store that sold his second Franco mask."

"We'll have to have an airtight case before arresting him. It's a good thing that we're not releasing the information to the public about our rapist using a mask," said Diego.

Marielena said, "OK. We know where he is now and where he is employed. We also know what he got his education in. What we need to prove is whether he was at all the other places where our M.O. rapes took place. Where did he get his education? What teaching jobs did he have prior to Madrid? Was he ever an actor? Could he have been the actor in Gernika? Would any other actor recognize him? Would his colleagues know when he took weekend vacations and where he went? We need to corroborate everything."

Diego added, "I think the first step would be to acquire a college record. From your timetable, he would have to have gone to college in the Basque country. We know a series of rapes occurred during that time frame. Rather than tip him off by asking him for any information or asking at the Carreras Universitarias de Bellas Artes en Madrid, let's use his name, plus police censorship, to check out the colleges in the Basque area that gives degrees in art. If it is art degrees that we're interested in, that's more up your alley to ask questions."

"Good idea, but we still need to establish that he definitely purchased a Franco mask."

"Why don't I take all the addresses of the possible sources for the mask. I'll call for a specific location or locations which have or have sold a Franco mask recently. Since there are so many places to start with, I'll contact my friends in Madrid. Maybe they can have someone on their force help me check out all the costume shops and theatrical stores. When I

Chapter 23

narrow down the list to those locations, I'll take the image that you recognize with me to visit the places to see if I can get a hit of purchaser identification. It's too bad we're located here in San Anton, not Madrid; and he lives in Madrid. We could get a search warrant and go to his residence to search for a Franco mask. Only the Madrid police can do that, but we don't want them to do that at this time because we'd basically be telling him that he is our suspect. He could have the mask hidden so well that we wouldn't find it on the first try. He'd lay low and we'd miss our chance to nail him. As it is, he doesn't suspect now that we're on to him. Maybe we'd better let that be the case until we have enough evidence to really get him arrested. Anyway, as I work on the mask sources, you contact whatever college or academy of art where he might have gone to get an art education. If you find a school, take a younger version of Villars' photograph and see if there's anyone still at the college who recognizes, or better yet remembers him," said Diego.

Marielena thought for a moment and then said, "What if I also went back to Gernika and check out a younger version of the photograph with the theater manager there to verify Villars was the actor playing Franco? If I have to go to the Basque area, I could kill two birds with one stone."

"Super idea. We have a lot of ground to cover, and we don't know how much time we have until he finds another victim."

Marielena reminded him, "Remember to cross off the two stores which I've already checked out."

~ ~

Chapter 24
Marielena Checks Colleges

Deciding not to give anything away that might tip off Professor Villars, Marielena Googled art colleges and universities in the Basque country. While there were numerous small academies and small art colleges, she looked at the names carefully. Only one university looked big enough to give credentials to an art professor needing the ability to move around from job to job with ease. The rapist had shown by his numerous rapes in different locations that he was readily able to find employment quickly and without difficulty.

The Campus De Bizkaia Public University in Leioa Barrio Sarriena was close to Bilbao. It fit her criteria for a large art university, and she decided to contact their Arte Ederrer Fakultakea and ask about records for a past student named Alejandro Villars. She tried to come up with an excuse, not including police business, which would allow her to ask about alumni there. Finally, with Diego's help, she decided to pretend she was one of his students who wished to plan a celebration of

The Urge

Villars' teaching abilities.

She contacted the art faculty and gave her a fictitious story. The receptionist in the art building looked at her computer list of past students at the school and found that, yes, Alejandro Villars was an alumnus. He had received outstanding grades and had graduated with honors.

Marielena then asked, "Are there any faculty members still on staff who would have had him in class or who would remember him? What about other students who would remember him and be able to share personal anecdotal experiences with him? I'd really like to get personal recollections, if possible."

"Oh, yes," replied the receptionist. "I believe Professor Mariano Luis Andujar Arroya Dies was his mentor; and you're in luck, he is still on our faculty."

"Oh, good," said Marielena. "Do you have contact information for him so that I can contact him directly?"

"Yes," replied the secretary. She gave Marielena both the professor's office telephone number and his email address.

Marielena thanked her profusely and then called the professor directly. At first, she thought about using the same ploy she had used with the secretary, but instead she introduced herself as a police detective wanting information. After introducing herself, she informed Professor Luis that what they were going to be discussing was to be kept completely secret as it might affect a police investigation. He said that he would cooperate completely but seemed to be taken aback somewhat and asked why the police was interested in him.

Marielena answered, "This concerns some crimes that were committed when our 'person of interest' was

Chapter 24

a student here and what he has been doing since." That seemed to placate the professor. She asked, "Do you remember a past student named Alejandro Villars?"

Professor Luis quickly responded, "Oh yes, I remember him quite well. He had a wonderful academic record. Yes, Yes - quite a superior student." He paused for a minute and then added, "Extremely introverted, quiet, and somewhat withdrawn as an individual though. I haven't had any contact with him for a number of years."

Marielena then switched tactics and started asking about Villars's art. "What sort of artworks did he produce as a student?"

Professor Luis thought for a moment and then spoke slowly, "His artwork was sometimes bizarre with abstract patterns and sometimes in non-harmonious colors. While he produced abstract art which sometimes does look bizarre, especially to those not of the art community, his artwork seemed different somehow to me. Almost grotesque. Far beyond the art of Picasso, Miro, Klee, or other abstractionists. Most of the faculty seemed to think everything he did was wonderful, but at the time when he was a student, abstract art was all the rage.

"I asked him once about it, and he just laughed and said, 'We all see things differently, don't we?' I never said anything to him again. I was afraid to stifle his creativity.

"I did, however, speak with his guidance counselor, who was another of his professors, who had degrees in both art and psychology. He agreed with me that he thought Alejandro was a disturbed young man. He had tried to get him into a counseling session with some of the other students. Alejandro had said at that time,

The Urge

'I don't need counseling. There is nothing wrong with me.' His counselor told me that he never brought the subject up with him again.

"Again, can I ask why the police are interested in him?"

"I find it interesting that Alejandro graduated from college without being in a counseling group. When I went to college, it was required. In answer to your question, I'm here about a very old case going back a long time, about the time Alejandro was in college there. We think he might have been involved. Actually, I'm calling now just to confirm that he did attend your college during a particular time frame."

Professor Luis paused questioningly when she said that, but he didn't respond in any way. While what she had told him was true, she felt she couldn't divulge anything more. She didn't tell the professor anything more about what they suspected of Villars's activities during college or his more recent activities. She thanked the professor and left.

Since Villars hadn't participated in any counseling sessions, she didn't feel she needed to pursue that line. She had established however that Villars had been in the area of the Basque country where and when rapes had occurred. She determined she should continue on to Gernika and see if the stage manager recognized the photographs which she and Diego had their computer expert make. She called the retired policeman, Señor Etxarrin to see if she could get the phone number and address of the production manager in Gernika and arrange to see him.

Señor Etxarrin said, "I'll contact him and set up an appointment and take you there. I've nothing better to do today, and I'd love to be there if he recognizes your suspect. It's been a long time for me to wait for

Chapter 24

a person to be identified as my cold-case rapist. Give me your number and I'll call you right back."

Marielena waited less than twenty minutes and her phone rang.

Señor Etxarrin asked her where she was so he could pick her up. Within an hour they were on their way to Gernika. One the way she filled him in on what she had just learned at the art college. He thought for a moment and then said, "So he's been at work raping women for almost twenty-five years and hasn't gotten caught. He is either extremely careful or he's been very lucky."

"Or both," replied Marielena.

"Oh, here we are," said Señor Etxarrin, "Now maybe we'll see if we can put another piece of the puzzle in place."

Marielena and Señor Etxarrin went into the Theatro de Gernika. A man came to meet them and Señor Etxarrin introduced him to Marielena. They walked to the production manager's office which had a large window. Marielena explained that they now had a person of interest who may have been the actor playing Franco in the play years ago. She said she knew that he had been in his teens when the play was conducted and that he had also been in that particular play. She asked, "Would you please look at a photo and see if, indeed, their suspect was that actor?"

Señor Garso, the production manager, took one look at the photo and exclaimed, "Yes, that's the man, but he was much younger."

Then Marielena showed him the photo of Henri.

Señor Garso said, "The age is about right, but the coloring is wrong - much too dark complected and

The Urge

dark eyes and hair. Are they related?"

Marielena then said, "Now look at this photo." She showed the digitally manipulated photo of Villars as a young man with the proper colored hair, eyes, and complexion.

Señor Garso said, "That is a perfect picture of the actor who played Franco. The colorations and age are just right. Again, is 'our' actor related to the other younger man?"

Marielena answered, "We believe they are father and son."

"They look exactly alike," said Señor Garso. "I'm so glad I could help you."

Marielena asked, "Could we have you sign a sworn affidavit to that effect?"

"Oh, yes," said Señor Garso. "I know that is the man who was in the play with me. I'd recognize him anywhere even though it was years ago. You know how young people idolize others who are better than they are. I'm afraid I was so in awe of his acting abilities that I idolized him. I thus have no doubt about who he was - or should I say, is?"

Retired policeman Señor Etxarrin and Marielena took Señor Garso to the local police station where he signed the necessary affidavit.

When Señor Etxarrin and Marielena left Gernika, they felt very confident and pleased with their afternoon's work.

Señor Etxarrin said to Marielena as they came back to Bilbao, "I'm so happy that you're getting the evidence to end this long nightmare of rapes. Too many women have suffered at the hands of this rapist. I'm glad I could be of assistance. This cold case has haunted me

Chapter 24

for so many years. When you actually arrest him and he is convicted, I can put these memories to rest."

Marielena reached over and patted his hand saying, "You've played a major part in this search. Thank you. I'll be in touch."

Señor Etxarrin let her out at the Bilbao bus station for her trip back to San Anton. With the affidavit and photos in her briefcase, Marielena heaved a huge sigh of relief. She knew that she had just added another major nail in Villars's coffin. Unfortunately, there was still a need for other information and nails to be added.

~ ~

Chapter 25
Diego's Search

While Marielena had gone to the Basque country to confirm where Villars had received his higher education and to establish where he was during his college years, Diego set out to connect Villars to the purchase of a Franco mask. At least they had checked Amazon and knew it wasn't the source of Villars' mask. Since Marielena had already checked out two of the thirty-four places, there were thirty-two to go. He looked at his half of the list. If he got lucky in his search, Marielena wouldn't have to contact her sixteen.

Using the internet to get phone numbers, Diego proceeded to call each establishment. On his thirteenth call, one to a theatrical warehouse supply store, he finally found what he had been searching for. Their answer was, "Yes, we have masks of the dictator Franco, but there hasn't been much demand for them. In fact, we thought about discontinuing them last year, but we still have an inventory of six or so."

Diego asked, "Have you sold any recently?"

The Urge

"Why yes, that's strange, but we did sell one about four weeks ago."

"Can I come and get some information about the purchase?"

"Yes, the salesperson who works our front desk is here every day from nine until one and then again from four to seven. I'm sure he could answer any of your questions. What is this about?"

Diego said quietly, "It's a matter of police business - if you could please keep that information quiet."

"Of course. I'll say nothing to anyone about it."

"Who should I ask for when I get to your warehouse?"

"Señor Lopez."

"And your name?"

"Señor Garcia, I'm the warehouse manager."

"Gracias," said Diego.

Knowing that he could drive to Madrid in an hour-and-a-half or, at most, two hours, Diego told Deputy Ortega that he would hopefully be back in approximately five hours. Diego went to his car and left San Anton for Madrid. As he drove, he considered how much he was going to tell the salesman when he arrived at the warehouse. He figured he would arrive at the warehouse about four o'clock when Señor Lopez started his afternoon work hours.

Diego actually arrived about fifteen minutes after four o'clock giving Señor Lopez time to settle into his job. Diego knew from experience that it takes people too much by surprise if you catch them before or minutes after they get to work. Usually, they are less cooperative then, than if you allow them to 'see you coming'.

Chapter 25

Approaching the salesman, he said, "Señor Lopez?"

"Yes," said the man. "What can I do for you for you?"

"I spoke with Señor Garcia yesterday. He said you had sold a Franco face mask recently."

"Why yes, that's true. We don't get much call for those masks anymore - there was a time, of course - but not now. That's probably the only one in the last five years that's been sold since I've been working here."

"I'm here to ask you about the person who purchased it." Diego showed him his police identification badge. "The matter is quite important but must be kept in strictest silence. You understand?"

"Oh - of course, yes," stammered Señor Lopez.

Whether he did or not, Diego couldn't decide; but he continued, "I assume it was a man who purchased the mask?"

"It was a man, and the mask was a complete head mask that pulls down over the head extending down to the shoulders. The entire head and neck are covered. Its bottom can be tucked into a shirt or jacket collar, and it isn't detectable just looking at the person. It really is quite life-like."

"Did the man tell you why he wanted the mask?"

"Yes. He said his mother, who will be turning ninety years old, is one of those people in our country who still revere Franco and his memory. He and his sister are planning a surprise birthday party for her, and he thought it would be fun to show up to the party dressed as Franco. He said he hoped his mother wouldn't die of fright, but he laughed really loudly and said, he could hardly wait to surprise her."

The Urge

"I see," said Diego. "Can you describe the man?"

"Yes - let's see. He was tall and slender. Very soft-spoken, polite. Medium brown hair, light hazel eyes, light complected."

Diego took the digitally manipulated picture from his jacket and asked, "Is this the man?"

"Yes, that's him."

"How did he pay for the mask?"

"Cash," replied Señor Lopez.

"So, you don't have a name? Or a credit card receipt?"

"No," said Señor Lopez.

"Would you sign this form that this photo is of the man who purchased the mask?"

"Of course."

The two of them approached the office of Señor Garcia. Diego asked if he would also sign the form as a witness. Diego wasn't going to have any slip-ups with evidence. This identification was too good and would be needed when the trial came up in a courtroom. Señor Lopez had identified Professor Villars as the person who had purchased the Franco mask.

As Diego drove back to San Anton, he mused that the noose was closing tighter around Villars's neck. It was too bad that Villars lived in Madrid instead of San Anton. If he lived in San Anton, he and his police force could have him under surveillance to see if they could catch him in the act. It would be difficult since they were such a small police department, but he would have managed somehow. If they were responsible, they would have him arrested and tried in San Anton.

Chapter 25

But with Villars living in Madrid, he and Marielena needed to report all their findings to the Madrid police. Any surveillance, arrest, and trial would, of course, take place in the Madrid police district by the Madrid police.

He and Marielena needed to be sure to have all the loose ends tied up before confirming to the Madrid police they had found the serial rapist. Once the news was released, he realized they both would have to be in Madrid for a number of days.

First, they would need to have at least one meeting, but possibly more, with the Madrid police commissioner, the police officers involved, any detectives that had worked the rape cases involved, the prosecuting attorney, and possibly others to present their case.

Second, they would both probably be subpoenaed to appear in court during a trial, especially Marielena. She had really done all the work on finding the rapist. Plus, she would be called as a witness too since she had been attacked and, for the grace of God and his own foresight in getting her self-defense classes, could easily have been one of Villars's rape victims.

He also needed to put his own police station in order so that they could be gone during that time. Deputy Ortego would be working a lot of overtime. There was a lot to do and probably not a lot of time to do it in. In the meantime, they ran the chance that Villars would find another victim.

He heaved a sigh when he considered the amount of planning that he and Marielena needed to do. He wondered what she had found out on her trip to the Basque country. He hoped she had encountered as much success as he had in his search today.

~~

Chapter 26
Missing Evidence

Diego and Marielena sat in her office looking at her charts, the map, the lists of victims, places and dates of all the rapes, characteristics of victims, descriptions of the rapist, number of interviews of victims, three samples of DNA, and the timelines of Villars's employment or education which she had compiled. They carefully went over all the evidence and discussed it. They knew they had lots of facts that could be used against their suspect. After a long discussion about what they had, however, they realized there were still a couple of bits of information needed to build a really solid case.

One of the missing puzzle pieces was an employment record for Villars in the Barcelona area. Where had he lived and worked in Barcelona before coming to Madrid? Obviously, they couldn't ask the professor himself, without tipping him off that he was under investigation. Where would an art professor garner employment in the Barcelona area? What art institutions hired professional art professors? The

The Urge

rapes in Barcelona fell into a timeframe between the Basque area where Villars had gone to college and Madrid where he was currently employed at the Carreras Universitarias de Bellas Artes. While they had clearly established his presence in the Basque area at the time of those rapes and in the Madrid area during the time of the current rapes, they needed to fill in the gap between these "two bookends". They needed to prove his employment and residence in Barcelona in order to establish him there during the time of the rapes in that area.

Marielena searched on line for art schools in Barcelona, Spain, and found four art schools where someone with the impeccable credentials of Professor Villars could possibly be employed: Universitat de Barcelona, Metáfora Studio Artes, Estudio Nómada Barcelona Artes Esculea on Carrer de Trafalgar, and Atelier Barcelona Academy of Art. She had the telephone numbers of all the schools but realized, even if she called, she'd probably have to go to Barcelona to get notarized copies of his employment records and, if possible, affidavits from other employees or staff members who might remember him.

At that point, Diego got a phone call from his friends in the Madrid police force. Detective Martinez asked how he and Marielena were progressing in their search for the rapist. He reported that the rapist had struck again in the old town of Madrid the night before. Diego asked the particulars of the case, putting the call on speakerphone so Marielena could also be part of the conversation. Detective Martinez told him the M.O. was identical to the list of cases on file for the rapist. The victim was a middle-aged woman who had gone to the all-night grocery near a bank where she had withdrawn money from an automatic street kiosk. Since she hadn't been robbed, the rapist was focused

Chapter 26

only on rape, not robbery.

Diego reported that he and Marielena had a suspect but needed one more bit of information to have all the evidence needed to arrest him. Their suspect lived in Madrid and would be under Madrid jurisdiction. Diego assured Detective Martinez that as soon as they could gather the needed information, he and Marielena would both come to Madrid and share all their evidence. Obviously, most of the recent rapes had occurred in and around the Madrid area, including this last rape. It would be the Madrid police and court system handling both the arrest and trial. He and Marielena would be present for that trial and act as witnesses for the prosecution. He told Detective Martinez that he was going to make sure to have his own police district and station in order before the trial so he and Marielena would be at their disposal whenever needed.

Detective Martinez said, "I'll report to my lieutenant and commissioner about your progress. Of course, we will be anxiously waiting to hear all your evidence. Please try to make that as soon as possible. These rapes have to stop. I think every woman in Madrid, in fact, most of Spain, is frightened, thinking she'll be the next victim."

Diego responded, "It won't be long. We're working on the last piece now. Do you want Marielena to come up to Madrid to interview this latest victim right away?"

"Not really. The scenario of the rape fits so well into the pattern which we've observed that she needn't make an extra trip. I'd rather she remains in San Anton working with you on whatever you've got going right now. I think at this point it would be time wasted. I'm sure, when you come to give us all the evidence you've collected, there will be time for her to add an interview with this new victim to your information. She'll only

The Urge

have to make one trip. Go ahead and pursue the last evidence you need first."

After Diego hung up, he and Marielena discussed this new case which she added to her list of victims with a note to have an interview with the victim whenever she went to Madrid. She and Diego divided the list of the four Barcelona art schools between them so they could start calling for information on Villars.

Diego had no success with his two, but Marielena on her first call, after identifying herself as a police detective, got an affirmative answer from the employment office of the Universitat de Barcelona. Yes, they had employed Professor Alejandro Villars Correao Castillo Bodega directly after his graduation from college. He hadn't been a full professor, only an associate professor, but he had received glowing praises from both his colleagues and his students. The university had been very sad to lose him when he had taken the job in Madrid, but they realized he was moving upward to a full professorship. They were happy he was doing so well for himself.

Marielena asked if they would email a notarized copy of his entire employment with them to her, and she gave the email address of the police station.

They were more than happy to oblige. In fact, they would have a copy notarized and email that copy immediately to her. Fortunately, the office had a notary sitting right there in their office.

Marielena turned to Diego and stated, "Well, within a short time we'll have everything we need. The university is emailing his work record here right away." She had only to wait a few minutes before her computer listed the email had been received. She clicked on the email, looked it over, and promptly sent it to her printer. It was perfect. Not only did it tie Villars

Chapter 26

to employment in Barcelona, but it had his residence address in that city. The employment filled in the total gap of time from his college graduation to his initial employment date in Madrid and covered all the time that rapes were occurring in the Barcelona area. They again reviewed all their evidence. They looked at their charts.

- For DNA evidence, there were (they needed Villars's sample – at arrest?):
    - Pubic hair from Maria Alvelar in Madrid
    - Skin cells from Marisol Huevos in Seville
    - Saliva cells from Henri and Helena
- List of Locations of Rapes and Timeline compared to Villars's age:
    - Irun – result Henri – Villars 15-16 years old?
    - San Sebastian Area – Villars in high school, approx. ....19-20?
    - Bilbao Area – Villars in college and in play in Gernika...25?
    - Barcelona Area – Villars' teaching college.... 26 to 39?
    - Madrid Area – Villars' teaching college .... 40 to 49?
- More files included:
    - Police Interviews: numerous women
    - Marielena's records of these interviews
    - Marielena herself – her recognition of Franco mask
- Photographs of Villars identified by:
    - Production manager in Gernika - affidavit
    - Salesman at Theatrical Warehouse - affidavit
    - Young victim in Toledo – witnessed by her mother in the hospital
    - Numerous victims during interviews with Marielena
    - Police records of rapes in locations

The Urge

- Cold case records from numerous locations
- Current case records from Madrid and surrounding areas
- Marked map of the locations of rapes:
  - By city
  - By date
  - By arrows showing the order in time

At last, after an hour of study, they looked at each other and smiled. Diego reached for the telephone and called Detective Martinez in Madrid. As he connected with his friend, he said, "We need to set up at date for us to come to Madrid and present."

"Fantastic," said José. "I relayed your message from our last telephone call to my superiors and they informed me that they would clear everything from their desks at any time you were finished with your investigation. We are really happy to learn we will be arresting someone in the very near future. How about coming to Madrid tomorrow? We can hardly wait."

Diego answered, "I'll finish my day preparing my office, and we'll be there." As he ended his call, he called for Deputy Ortega to come to his office to assume the reins of control as he and Marielena would be leaving for Madrid first thing in the morning. He was glad he'd given Deputy Ortega a heads-up the previous day as to what was going to be happening.

~ ~

Chapter 27
Barcelona

The day had been extremely hot. Madrid's street shimmered in the sun. Villars remembered a similar day in Barcelona when he had lived there. There hadn't been a breeze to be found anywhere. Everyone tried to find some shade - any shade. If they had to go somewhere and they had to walk, they would cross the street to be in the shade either under the trees or under a building's shade. The Spanish "sol o Sombra" prevailed everywhere. If you were going to the bullfights, you were more than happy to pay almost twice as much for a Sombra seat. If you were parking your car, even for a few hours, you would choose a narrow street where your car would be shaded. Regardless, your car would be hot when you returned to it, but you could touch the door handles to open the door and ease yourself into a semi-hot seat if it had been in the shade. People wanted cold drinks - anything cold - cold beer, cold sangria, cold water - and especially cold food. Some tourists had not prepared for the heatwave and became dehydrated,

The Urge

passing out in the streets. It seemed the entire city was a cacophony of ambulance sirens retrieving the fallen.

Professor Villars remembers that day clearly. He had been experiencing "the urge" all week; and, even though he doubted he'd get any satisfaction, he had walked quickly from his job at the Universtat de Barcelona to his apartment. Like everyone else, he chose the shady sides of the boulevard, main street, and side streets to get there, even if it meant a longer walk. By the time he reached the apartment building, his shirt was clinging to his body as though he had glued it on.

He really loved his job and this city, especially the city. It had so many beautiful and unique sites to see from the fantastic harbor on the glistening, blue waters of the Mediterranean to Monastir de Montserrat in the mountains with its glistening gold and religious paintings. He loved walking down La Rambla to the waterfront and its statue of Christopher Columbus. La Rambla was the perfect street for strolling, buying flowers in the vending stalls, and people watching, really "potential victim" watching. The city had the most glorious art too, and much of it was due to the artist, Gaudi. There was his La Segrada Familia, his Casa Batilló, his Casa Milá, and his Parc Guell. With his own love of abstract art, Gaudi was his guide to beauty.

When he had graduated from the Campus de Bizkaria Public University and had applied for jobs, he had been very fortunate to find employment immediately in such a fine institution as the Universitat de Barcelona. The interview had gone very smoothly, and the admissions board had been impressed with his college resumé and his portfolio. One of their senior faculty members in the art department had recently

Chapter 27

retired and they were anxious to fill the vacant position. The professor whom they were replacing had been teaching art history, oil painting, and art theory. He was an abstract artist and so was Villars, which made the appointment every sweeter. Villars seemed to be the perfect candidate for the position. They couldn't offer him a full professorship because of his recent graduation and lack of teaching experience, but they did offer him an associate professorship which could, after a few years, be easily upped to a full professorship if he worked as well as they thought he might.

Villars had jumped at the offer. It was an offer much better than anything else offered to him by other universities. It was a much better offer than his fellow graduates were getting.

He had settled right in at the university quite easily; and, for a while, he was so busy that "the urge" hadn't taken over his life. Soon though, he started the search for locations in the city where he might satisfy his needs. He knew, ultimately, he would have to rape again. He had wanted to be ready. He had been faced with a new unknown city, unknown neighborhoods, unknown streets, and unknown alleys. He discovered so many excellent hunting areas that over the next few years, his victims were such that he could relax, enjoy his job, and his students while feeling perfectly safe.

The one night, however "the urge" was so strong he knew he had to "have" someone - he really didn't care who. Because of the oppressive heat of that day and evening, he might have slim pickings for candidate victims, but he prepared as usual - rag, condom, rubber gloves, and Franco mask. He decided to concentrate his search in an area northwest of the harbor and La Rambla. It was in an older part of town near the Plaza de Toro (bullfighting ring) and within a kilometer of his

The Urge

apartment. Narrow streets and still narrower and dark alleys wound through that part of the downtown. He had a mental map of the area since he loved to walk down to the harbor.

At last, he found a place that looked as though one building was totally deserted, another had very few windows on the alleyway, and there were several streets that converged, giving him lots of choices for a getaway. As if by some prompting, a young woman entered the alley from one of the converging streets. He had hidden close to one of the buildings with few windows in an especially dark shadow. As she approached, he donned his mask and slipped on the rubber gloves. When she passed him, he reached out, grabbed her, and stuffed the rag into her mouth. All seemed to go well until she tried to fight. Even then he subdued her, slipped on the condom, and raped her. The real problem arose when, as he finished, she had gathered her strength and kicked out. Instead of connecting with him, her foot hit a pile of cans that had been stacked next to one of the trash bins. The cans fell with a clatter, rolling and bouncing, and colliding with others and with some precariously stacked boxes and jars. The noise was deafening. As he hit the woman to knock her out and pushed her away from him and further into the shadows, a window opened right above his head, a light came on, and a woman yelled, "What's going on down there? What are you doing?" She pushed the window further open and shone a flashlight directly at his face. He then heard her yell, "Louis, call the police. There's a man standing right below our window."

Villars moved quickly, removed the rag, stuffed his full condom into it making a ball, and walked away from the scene. A block later he removed the mask and crammed it into his pocket. He still had the rag

Chapter 27

and its contents in his hand when he walked from the intersection into one of the streets, one which would be in the direction of his apartment. He was so flustered he forgot he still carried the balled-up rag.

At that point, things went from bad to worse. Two policemen came running up to him and shone their flashlights in his face.

One asked, "What is your name?"

Thinking quickly, he answered, "My name is Carlos Ortega".

"Where do you live?"

Villars pointed to a building a little further down the street and answered, "Down there".

"What are you doing out here and what's that in your hand?"

"I'm trying to take a walk to cool off. Oh, this, it's a handkerchief which I've been using to wipe away my sweat." As if to prove a point, he wiped his brow with the rag, hoping the condom stayed inside. It did, to his relief.

"Have you seen anyone or heard anything unusual?"

"Not really. I've only been out here for a few minutes. My apartment doesn't have air conditioning and it's cooler out here."

They again pointed the flashlight at his face. One of the policemen said, "This can't be the guy. We're looking for an almost bald guy with a mustache."

"He's the right height though."

Villars then said, "A man about my height just ran past me. I think he was bald. I didn't see him clearly enough to see if he had a mustache, but he was bald."

The Urge

"Which way did he go?"

"That way!" Shouted Villars, pointing in the direction opposite from his intended one.

The police ran off, yelling back to him, "Thank you, Señor Ortega.

He promptly walked as quickly as possible in the opposite direction. He wanted to run, but running people attracts attention. Several blocks later realizing he still grasp the rag with its rape contents in his hand, he deposited it in a trash bin. He tried to stay in dark alleys as much as he could during his entire walk home. It seemed to take him forever to reach his apartment building.

Unlocking his apartment, he almost fell through the door. His knees were shaking, he was sweating profusely and felt sick to his stomach. Within minutes he was kneeling beside the commode retching up everything which he had consumed that day. When he finished, he took a cool shower, dried himself off, and sat down with his head in his hands. He had almost gotten caught. Looking back, he realized the police hadn't asked for ID, they hadn't frisked him, and they had believed his lie about who he was, where he lived, and that he'd seen another man. It took him hours to get to sleep. He relived everything which had happened that night. He told himself he would have to be vigilant to avoid policemen because he might run into the ones who had seen him. He would have to avoid that part of town. He would have to curtail raping women. He was in trouble. Finally, he slept.

The next morning on the way to the university he purchased a newspaper. On the front page was an article that described the rape which had occurred the previous night. The words leaped from the page saying "The Barcelona police force stated that like last night's

Chapter 27

rape, many of the recent rapes in the Barcelona area have followed the same scenario, so we are assuming the city has a serial rapist at large. Women are urged to use extreme caution when going to and from work and to avoid going out alone at night. We are encouraging anyone with knowledge of last night's attack to come forward with that information. We are looking for a particular man of interest, a Carlos Ortega, who may have been near the scene."

At that point, even though he continued to read the rest of the article, the words had little meaning and his mind went blank. Villars found a park bench and sat. Again, his knees were shaking, and he felt extremely weak. He had almost been caught. Much as he liked his job and this city, he knew he must move on. Thankfully, it was good the end of term was so close. He must find another job far from Barcelona; he must refrain from further rapes or rape in a place at a distance from the city, and he must start an immediate search for new employment. He wouldn't tell anyone he was leaving until he had a place to go - but he had to leave Barcelona.

Instead of working on his lesson plans when he reached his university office, he started his job search.

Two weeks later he received the job offer from Madrid and three weeks later he finished the spring term, tendered his resignation, packed his few belongings, and moved. All his friends expressed regret that he was leaving and wished him well. No one connected his leaving with the cessation of rapes in Barcelona. He was very lucky.

~ ~

Chapter 28
At the Madrid
Police Headquarters

As Diego and Marielena drove to Madrid the next morning with all their charts, lists, DNA samples, and marked map, Diego said to Marielena, "You realize that you are going to be making our presentation at this meeting? You are the one who has done all the work. I've only helped at points along the way, but this is 'your baby'. I'll introduce you, but you will need to be the one doing the presenting."

"Oh, I'm not sure I can do that," Marielena exclaimed.

"Why not?" asked Diego. "You know the facts and the evidence better than I do."

"What shall I say?"

"You just start by telling them what got you interested in this search from the very beginning. You go through the cases one by one, starting with the current rapes in the Madrid area. Tell about your own attack, what clues you had, and how you surmised the rapist wore a mask. How you put two-and-two together

The Urge

to compile what the rapist looked like and how your recollections and the other victims' descriptions created the sketch. How all his victims resembled each other, including your own description. How he is looking for a particular type of victim. How we saw the Franco documentary and you realized the rapist wore a Franco mask. About your search of rape records from various locations, mapping them, and tracing these records back in time. You can easily tell how you mapped the rapes in order, developed a timeline, and found witnesses through cold-case files of rapes. You should have no problem describing Helena and Henri. Plus, you'll tell them about the DNA samples, even the ones which will link the rapist to his own son. You'll tell them that when the rapist is apprehended, they will need to obtain a DNA sample from him to get a match with the samples we already have. What are you worrying about?

"You have the best handle on this case. Better than I do. Calm down. If you start stumbling in your presentation, I'll insert facts as you go along. Remember, I'll always have your back. It really ought to be 'a piece of cake' for you."

Marielena thought to herself, "I've really gotten myself into it now. Thank God I have Diego to back me up.

Not knowing how long the Madrid police department would want to meet with them, they had packed two overnight bags with clothing for approximately three days in the trunk of their car. If they had to stay more than one day, they were prepared.

Reaching Madrid, they drove to the police station, parked in the parking lot, unloaded all their evidence, and carried everything inside. They left their personal luggage locked in the trunk. They had called ahead

Chapter 28

indicating their approximate arrival time, so they were immediately greeted by two police detectives in the main lobby. Since Marielena had worked with both of them before when she had come to Madrid to interview victims and make her sketch of the rapist, she was greeted as warmly as if she were a member of their own police station. One of the detectives, José Martinez, had known Diego previously and had been their contact person, so there was only one introduction made, Diego to the second detective, Detective Rafael Bosques, before the four of them walked back to a huge meeting room.

Looking around the room, Marielena realized her audience was not only large, but the large number present indicated the importance of her investigation. Here were the police commissioner, his lieutenant, the police officers who had been called to rapes, the detectives who had investigated rapes in Madrid, and a secretary to take notes of the proceedings. In all there were over twenty-five people present, including herself and Diego. She took a deep breath to steady herself.

The commissioner himself welcomed them after being introduced by Detective Martinez. He had not been in charge of the Madrid office when Diego had worked there.

Diego asked for help in putting the map and charts on the walls; then, he stated that while he had helped in the search for the serial rapist, the real work had been carried out by his part-time deputy, Marielena Cortez-Rivera.

He added, "Marielena just happens to be my wife and an artist, as some of you already know." Some of those present smiled at his remark. Diego continued, "Since she carried out this investigation from the beginning and knows the facts better than I, it is only fitting that she, not I, bring you up-to-date on how she proceeded in the entire process, how she arrived at her facts, how she corroborated our findings, and how she now has confirmed the identity of the rapist." He directed their attention to Marielena, and said, "Marielena, please proceed."

Marielena stood and went to the front of the room. She said, "I appreciate all the help which I received from Detective Martinez and Detective Bosques when I came to interview victims. Without these victims' accounts, I might never have started putting all the initial pieces of this puzzle together." She directed their attention to the two detectives and started clapping for them. The others who were present joined her. She continued, "As rape reports were issued from your department, I concluded that there seemed to be a pattern to how and who was raped, when the rapes occurred, and where the rapes occurred. I began by making a list of the victims, a list of where the rapes occurred, a list of times when the rapes occurred, and a list of how these rapes occurred. After discussing the information which I had collected with my husband and boss, Commissioner Diego Rivera, we concluded we needed more information from the victims themselves. That's when he contacted you and I came to Madrid to interview the victims. Please direct your attention to the chart with the list of victims. At the bottom of that list, you will see the enumeration of the victims which have occurred in the Madrid area and surrounding areas over the last four years. These victims were where I began my investigation. Notice I still need to interview your latest victim from two days past."

She gave her audience a few minutes to look at the chart. Continuing, she said, "All the victims from this list and several more from surrounding areas

Chapter 28

confirmed that the rapist was tall, quite muscular, physically strong, soft-spoken, polite, and looked familiar. As I interviewed them, I was able to compose a sketch of his approximate features. Almost all the victims stated that the rapist's eyes were different than my sketch but couldn't quite tell what was wrong with my initial sketch. I, myself, when he attacked me during the time when I was in Madrid working with art students, saw the rapist and also thought he looked familiar.

"I did have one bit of information that they lacked. During my attack, I had keys in my hand and knew I had cut his face from left eye to chin; however, he made no sound of pain nor outcry from that supposed injury. I deduced that he had been wearing a mask and I had damaged the mask, not his face. After watching a documentary of Francisco Franco, I realized the rapist had been wearing a mask of Franco during his rapes. All his victims had not associated the face of a deceased person with a present-day rapist. When I later showed photos of Franco to them, they all recognized that, indeed, the rapist looked like Franco."

Marielena directed their attention to a large photograph of Franco which they had brought with them and tacked up on the wall and said, "Let me digress for just a minute and direct your attention to the map of rapes and compare it to the chart with the list of dates when rapes were done. Please notice, that dates for rapes in the city of Madrid occurred for the most part on weekdays, and dates for rapes in the surrounding areas of Salamanca, for instance, occurred on weekends. From this, I surmised the rapist had to be living and working in the city of Madrid.

"I still had no idea what his occupation was or his education or his background. I speculated that he might have been committing rapes prior to the current

The Urge

ones in Madrid so I went to the newspapers and found that rapes had occurred in the areas of Barcelona, Bilbao, and San Sebastian. Commissioner Rivera and I checked out the actual rape accounts with the corresponding police forces and the M.O. of almost all the rapes, especially their cold cases, were the same. This indicated the rapist had been at work for almost a quarter-century. He had never been caught because when it became clear he might be discovered, he simply moved on."

Marielena pointed to the chart of the rapist's assumed age and place of the rapes.

"Our break happened when I made the assumption there might be a reason why a Franco mask had been chosen for a disguise. In a list of cold-case rapes in the Bilbao region, a retired police officer remembered there had been a theatrical production in Gernika where a Franco mask had been used by an actor. He followed up that clue for me, but the theatrical records had been incinerated in a fire. The production manager remembered the actor and could give us an approximate age of the rapist at that time. Extrapolating from that time, I could determine the ages of the rapist when committed the rest of his rapes, and approximately what he might have been doing other than raping in those time-frames. For example, when he was in college or when he was in high school, or when he was working corresponded to those times. I then started looking for specific rapes in those locations and got lucky. One rape, note the first victim listed on the chart, occurred in a pueblo called Irun. In that rape, the victim had become pregnant. With the help again from the San Sebastian police department, both the victim and the resultant son were found. We have DNA saliva samples from both, but we also have something else. We have an actual

Chapter 28

description of the rapist, prior to his use of a mask. The son, Henri, was said to look exactly like the rapist, who would have been his father. We took photos and digitally manipulated them by changing hair, skin, and complexion colorings. As a result, we used those to identify the rapist. Several victims have corroborated our findings. Please look at these new photos. Diego, will you please put those up? The rapist is Professor Alejandro Villars, an art professor, right here in your city."

Everyone in the audience strained to look at the new photos as Diego hung them on the wall.

Marielena continued, "We know his address and his place of employment, both of which are here in Madrid. From the recent rapes, I concluded the rapist had to be a resident of Madrid and Professor Villars is such a resident. Because of his current residence and the number of recent rapes recorded. he is therefore in your jurisdiction. We are not members of your police force so we will leave it up to you to possibly put him under surveillance, arrest him, and try him for his criminal rapes. Unfortunately, some of them are now so old as to probably not be able to be charged, having reached the statute of limitations. We have DNA samples from Seville and Madrid, as well as from Irun. We do not yet have a sample of Professor Villars's DNA, but that can be obtained, with his fingerprints, upon his arrest. If what I think and propose is true, you will find a match to all the rapes that are on the chart that hangs there. Commissioner Rivera and I will help you in any way which we can to bring this man to justice, including being witnesses for you in a trial proceeding."

As Marielena walked back to her seat, she received a standing ovation from all present. The Madrid police commissioner stood and thanked her for all her hard

The Urge

work and vowed to bring Professor Villars in before the day was over. He stated that with all the evidence which Marielena had, he didn't feel it necessary to put Villars under surveillance as it would only give Villars time to find another victim.

~ ~

Chapter 29
The Arrest

Professor Villars had been feeling "the urge" grow stronger over the past week. He hadn't read any news reports or seen any television programs concerning his rapes for several weeks. In that time, he hadn't been active either; but, prior to the last few weeks, reports had been rampant. He assumed this reporting meant that the police weren't any closer to discovering who he was. The old adage "no news is good news" gave him a sense of security.

Maybe it was time he should "go hunting" again. He prepared accordingly before going to work. He had scouted out an area near the metro station and knew of an unlit alley two blocks from a side street filled with tapas bars and a few hotels which catered to tourists. It was perfect for his purposes. If he got lucky, he'd have his "urge" satisfied tonight.

All day as he taught his classes, he could hardly concentrate. To make his day easier he assigned his students projects which were primarily self-directed

The Urge

so he himself had little to do other than monitor their progress and watch. Such lessons were his "fallback system" for easy days when "the urge" took over his life. After his last class, several students stayed back to ask specific questions concerning their projects. He was almost abrupt with them, but he realized he still had plenty of time to answer questions adequately and get home well before dark. He even had time to grab a quick bite to eat on the way home. The students thanked him for his help and told him how grateful they were for taking some of his personal time.

He stopped at a small bar near his apartment which he frequented and ordered calamari, a tortilla, and a beer. The bartender, whom he knew, tried to talk to him, but he explained that he was anxious to get home and prepare his lessons for the next day. While it was a lie, the bartender didn't know the difference and sympathized with him that one's work never seemed to get finished.

As the daylight faded, he walked to the last block to his apartment. As he entered the apartment house, a police car drove by, but he wasn't worried. There was a policeman he knew who lived three blocks away and always drove down his street on the way home.

When he got into his apartment, he changed into a black long-sleeved tee and black pants. The pants were of a cargo variety with deep side pockets where he placed his condom, rubber gloves, rag, and mask. With the weather turning much warmer, he wouldn't be wearing a jacket this evening. Much too warm. Probably too warm for a long-sleeved tee too; but, as the evening became cooler, he wouldn't look too inappropriately dressed. He looked around and took a deep breath. Now to the hunt!

As he walked toward the front door, there was a

Chapter 29

knock on it. He thought, what now? Who's going to ruin my evening? Whomever it is, I hope they leave quickly. Maybe it's someone who's lost and knocking on my door by mistake. Whatever! He opened the door. Standing outside were two men. He looked at them expectantly and said, "Yes?"

One of them said, "Alejandro Villars?"

He answered saying, "Yes, I'm he."

"Professor Villars, you are under arrest!"

"What for? I've done nothing wrong. I'm sure you have the wrong man."

"No, you are being arrested for committing rapes. Please turn around." As that was said, both men reached out. One started to frisk him and the other took his arms and placed handcuffs on his wrists.

All Villars could do was stare over his shoulder in disbelief, as they found his Franco mask, rag, rubber gloves, and condom in his pockets. There was no way to argue at this point. He knew his life had caught up with him. He knew they had him cold.

One of the men said, "It looks like you've been caught red-handed. Also looks like our timing is perfect to save some poor woman from being another of your victims."

Even as Villars sputtered in indignation, claiming this had to be some sort of a mistake, in his heart he knew that somehow, somewhere he had made a big mistake. He had to have slipped up some time so that the authorities had found him out and were now in the process of "taking him in".

He knew he had to keep his mouth shut until he realized what they knew, how much they knew, and how they knew what they knew. In the meantime, he

The Urge

would profess innocence and hope for the best - that they knew little, that they were guessing, and that they had no witnesses with incriminating evidence.

~ ~

Chapter 30
In Jail

Professor Villars was totally disoriented. Locked in a cell, clothed in prison garments, he sat on the edge of a bunk bed with his head in his hands. It all seemed like a nightmare. He'd been handcuffed, read his rights, taken to jail, fingerprinted, mouth swabbed for a DNA sample, rape kit used on him, pubic hairs removed, and head shaved. All before he was allowed to shower, given prison clothes, and locked in a cell.

His personal effects - wallet, wristwatch, coins, paper money, his Franco mask, rag, condom, rubber gloves, and street clothes had been inventoried and taken away. An officer asked him if he had a lawyer or if he could afford a lawyer. When he said that he didn't and couldn't, he was told that he would be assigned a lawyer by the district. He had tried to ask what evidence they had against him.

The answer was, "Plenty!"

As he had looked at them with an expectant expression on his face, he had been told nothing else.

The Urge

Nothing was enumerated as to how many cases he faced nor whom his accusers were.

As he sat there, he wondered how they had finally found him. He had been so careful all these years.

Which rape did they have evidence for? He assumed it had to be only one where he had slipped up; but which one? What kind of a mistake had he made?

Since this was the Madrid police station, maybe it was one of the Madrid ones. Or, was he here simply because he lived here in Madrid, and it was easier for the Madrid police to arrest someone in the capital city of Madrid.

No, wait - when they had arrested him, they had said rapes, plural. At least they hadn't said murder. Maybe they hadn't made the connection to the university student who he had killed as well as raped.

Which rapes? He had made up his mind not to offer any information to anyone about anything. Until he had a better idea, he'd be silent. No use admitting to anything. Anything at all.

After an hour of waiting, the lights dimmed, and the jail became quiet. No one had come near him. He didn't even have a cellmate to ask anything from. It was if the world had stopped. He finally laid down on the lower bunk where he had been sitting and covered himself with the thin blanket provided to prisoners. At least it was warm enough that this one blanket would keep him warm. If not, there was another blanket on the upper bunk, and no one was using it. He hoped tomorrow he would know more. Unfortunately for him, sleep wouldn't come. He tried to force himself to sleep, but the uncertainty in his mind kept him turning and tossing restlessly.

He'd always had trouble sleeping, even when he was

Chapter 30

a little boy. His sleeplessness now was different from then, but also somehow the same. It was a mixture of unknowing what was happening, being unsure of himself, and panicking that he wouldn't please people or succeed.

He had realized at an early age he was an unwanted child. His older brother seemed to be the perfect offspring, the offspring that his parents always had wanted. Luis could do no wrong. He was at the top of his class academically, he was the super athlete, and his personality seemed so magnetic as to attract both young and old alike. He had never lacked for friends. When Luis was little, his teachers raved about how smart he was, and his parents bragged when he brought home papers showing high marks. Luis could run faster than anyone his age and became an expert soccer player. Luis could always find someone who wanted to play with him. As he aged, not only did he have lots of male friends, but girls swooned over him. He never lacked for dates. Luis grew up a handsome, muscular, and confident person who was the envy of everyone in their community. He was his parent's pride and joy. His father always took Luis everywhere he went, introducing him to friends, neighbors, or anyone who just happened to be around. It was like Luis was dad's alter ego. Their mother beamed whenever Luis was around.

Villars' little sister, Lola, was not only the baby of the family but the favorite of both his father and his mother. Besides being "daddy's little girl", she was Mama's companion, confidant, and friend. She could do no wrong. Even when she did goof up and do something bad, excuses were made for her. "After all, she's just a baby and doesn't know any better." Lola was pretty with large dark eyes, luxurious dark hair that fell in ringlets almost to her waist, and a

The Urge

smile that lit up her whole face. Her eyes were bright and twinkling, sometimes mischievously, but usually as though someone had just told a joke and she had enjoyed hearing it. Their grandparents also doted on her because she was the only girl in the immediate generation. All the other sons and daughters no girls, only boys. Being the only girl put her in a different category, but also being so cute didn't hurt.

And then, there was himself, Alejandro Villars. When he had been younger, he was scrawny, his face had pimples, his hair seemed untamable, and he was extremely shy and timid. To add to all these, his mannerisms seemed effeminate. He spoke so softly that people had to strain to hear him whenever he did speak. Being so shy he seldom spoke; but, when he did speak, he almost stuttered. He was everything opposite of his brother, Luis. If his parents had expected a second son to be another Luis, they had been severely disappointed. He wasn't at all athletic and he had a difficult time with schoolwork, at least through all the lower grades. He didn't seem to be able to read and write well. Truly, his parents had nothing to brag about him. On the contrary, since he could do nothing to please them, they constantly criticized him. When he brought home bad grades, his father beat him with a belt. His mother made sure to make his life unpleasant in other ways. She gave his siblings the best foods, made sure they always had new clothes and spent time with them. The only time he had spent with his mother was when the other children were also with him. They never had any one-on-one time at all. His mother had nothing for him but derision. She said he must be gay to be so effeminate; his love of art and music was womanish, and he couldn't play soccer.

"Why can't you be a *real* boy and play sports, like Luis?"

Chapter 30

She told her friends and neighbors that she loved all her children, but he knew better. Many nights he had cried himself to sleep or lay in bed for hours wondering what was wrong with him? What would become of him if he was such a loser? What could he do to be accepted? How would he ever amount to anything? Why was he beaten by his father, but his brother and sister weren't? The worry and anxiety dogged him every day, but particularly every night. He needed sleep, but it did not always come.

His situation became even worse when he finally reached his teen years and started to shoot up in height and put on weight. His mother complained then that he was eating them out of house and home. Luis had eaten a lot too, but by that time he was old enough and had moved away. Since Luis wasn't eating there anymore, his mother had forgotten how much he had eaten. His mother kept insisting he'd never amount to anything. Even though he was way younger than his brother, she kept asking when he was going to leave. He was tired of looking at him and couldn't stand to have him around all the time.

At school, however, he had found a teacher who he liked and who encouraged him to do better. He started studying harder. Other teachers also discovered that a little praise when a long way and they started encouraging him too. In fact, he improved so much, that his grades earned him a scholarship to the art school at university. Even that wasn't good enough for his parents. They continued to argue about him. In his last two years of high school, his father finally tried to defend him, but by that time, it was too late. The damage had been done.

When he did go to college, he still had difficulty sleeping. His constant worry about whether he'd succeed in school and whether he would be able to

The Urge

support himself continued to plague him. After he had started raping girls more frequently, he worried if there was something wrong with him. He knew he didn't think of women or behave with women as he knew other men did. The professor in college, who had wanted him to enter counseling, had prompted a whole series of sleepless nights.

Now here he found himself in jail and again sleepless. What did they know? Was being in prison going to be his future? Uncertainty.

At last, toward morning he drifted off into a dream-filled unconsciousness of reliving one rape scene after another. Somewhere he'd made horrible mistakes, even though he couldn't remember a single time when he hadn't been extremely careful.

The guards came through about six in the morning. A loudspeaker told all prisoners to stand by their cell doors for a march to breakfast. After several minutes there was an alarm and their prison doors slid open automatically. He decided he'd be the model prisoner and follow all instructions and do what the other prisoners did, too. No use causing himself any more trouble than he was already in. He watched the other prisoners as they left their cells and stood near the cell doors. He did the same.

The guards marched all the prisoners single file to the prison dining room where they were served breakfast which lasted exactly thirty minutes before they were marched back to their cells. He knew it was thirty minutes because the wall clock in the dining room chimed at exactly thirty minutes before the guards came in to collect them.

After being in charge of his own life for so long, he quickly realized what he was experiencing today would be his life for a long time if he was sentenced.

Chapter 30

He wasn't sure he'd be able to endure it. Why hadn't he ever thought ahead far enough to picture what would happen if he were ever caught? Maybe he had never really thought the authorities would catch on to him? Who knew?

Later in the morning a guard came for him and took him to an interrogation room. Seated at the table was a small man in a suit and tie. He introduced himself as Señor Yugo Contreras, his court-appointed lawyer. He assured Professor Villars that he would do whatever he could to clear his name, but he seriously doubted he would be able to do much more than reduce his sentence which the court would give him.

Villars asked, "What do you mean?"

"Your DNA sample, which was taken yesterday matches three rape cases. Also, when you were arrested, you were in possession of a Franco mask that has been linked to numerous rapes, both here in Madrid and elsewhere. I'm assuming you will plead guilty to all these cases?"

"Definitely not!" Said Professor Villars. "I just purchased the Franco mask as a surprise for my mother's birthday party. I even told the salesman at the time of purchase what I had bought it for.

"As far as rapes, I don't know what you're talking about. I'm a respected faculty member of the Carreras Universitarias de Bellas Artes here in Madrid. I have no idea why I've been arrested. They must have mistaken me for someone else. I'm going to plead not guilty to anything they accuse me of. And that's final. I'm innocent!"

Señor Contreras sat back in his chair and folded his arms across his chest. He looked directly into Professor Villars' eyes and said very slowly, "I don't believe you;

The Urge

but, if that's your story, I'll try to defend you."

"That's my position," said Professor Villars. "I'll stick to it to whatever end we come to." He reminded himself that he'd gotten by for years without being caught. He had absolutely no criminal record. Not even a traffic ticket. Surely, they couldn't know everything. Maybe this lawyer could suggest that what they had was only circumstantial evidence. He was somewhat worried about the DNA though. He'd find a way to bluff through that though.

Señor Contreras said, "I need you to tell me about yourself so I can prepare some sort of defense for you."

Professor Villars smiled and asked, "What do you want to know?"

"Let's start with your employment record."

"Currently I'm a full professor of art at the Carreras Universitarias de Bellas as I mentioned previously. Before that, I was an associate professor of art in Barcelona at the Universitat de Barcelona. Before that, I was a college student at the Campus De Bizkaia Public University in Leioa Barrio Sarriena, which is close to Bilbao. I live in Madrid near the university which is where they arrested me yesterday."

Señor Contreras then asked, "Do you have friends or colleagues, who can vouch for your innocence?"

"They and any of my students can certainly vouch for my hard work, good reputation, love of my students, and expertise in the field of art and teaching. You can go to the university and ask anyone there. I also have several neighbors whom I have good relationships and dealings with. Even ask my department head at the university. I'm always on time, have a good work ethic, and never am absent. Just ask them. I'm not a criminal."

Chapter 30

"The police department officers tell me they have evidence of you being a serial rapist. Is there any truth to that?"

"I've already told you that I don't know what they're talking about. I think they have the wrong man."

"They showed me a Franco mask which they took from you when you were arrested. The serial rapist whom they've been looking for has been using a Franco mask to disguise himself during his rapes."

"It wasn't me."

"You realize if you're not honest with me, I don't have much of a chance to defend you?"

"You have nothing to defend me against. I'm not a rapist. You'll see. They can't prove I'm the man they're looking for."

Señor Contreras stood to leave, saying, "I hope that's the case because the court will start selecting jurors tomorrow. This is one trial that will not be postponed. The whole of Spanish citizenry is anxious to put this notorious rapist away for a long time and to stop looking over their shoulders at night in fear. The prosecution will do everything in its power to end this trial as soon as possible.

"Incidentally, if you need to speak to me, all my contact information is here at the jail since I'm court-appointed. All you have to do is ask to see me and I'll be here. You know, if, just if you remember something important to tell me, you need to tell me."

Shaking his head, Señor Contreras walked to the door, opened it, and signaled to the guard that Professor Villars was ready to be taken back to his cell. He knew his client was lying but had no way to prove it. He realized this was one case he would lose in the

The Urge

end. While he hated to lose cases, he was perfectly content to see the guilty convicted. And he knew in his heart that Professor Villars was guilty.

~ ~

Chapter 31
Juror Selection &
Trial's Beginning

The courtroom was practically empty. One by one potential jurors were brought in, questioned, and either dismissed completely or told to go home, pack enough clothing for a week of jury duty, and return that evening to be sequestered for the entire trial period. Of the forty prospective jurors initially, twenty had been dismissed almost immediately. Five of the women had themselves either been raped or molested, eleven of the men knew women who had either been raped or molested, and four of them cited business, age, physical infirmities, or religious reasons as excuses for not being able to serve on a jury. It took the entire day to arrive at a jury of nine with five alternates. The questioning seemed to go on endlessly. The judge was already tired, and the actual trial hadn't even begun.

As the rest of the potential jurors were finally dismissed and left the courtroom to go home, the prosecuting attorney, Señor Victor Ventura said to his associate, Señor Carlos Rios, "This trial will be a circus for the press and a disaster for the defense. We need

The Urge

to keep this a real win for all Villars' victims. I'm not sure why he's even claiming his innocence with all the evidence we have against him, but we'll see what his lawyer tries to prove in the next few days."

The next morning as soon as the courtroom doors opened, curious residents of Madrid pushed and shoved their way to obtain a seat for the first day of the trial. Many were local Madrid women who had been living in fear for four years that they might be the rapist's next victim. Not only were they anxious to see what the rapist looked like, but they needed to hear how he had eluded detection and apprehension for such a long time.

There were no women from other areas of Spain in the audience because the police had decided not to leak Villars' entire criminal past and areas of criminal activities to the press. The police had decided to share that information with the public only during the trial itself. News reports had only given a brief synopsis of the rapist, saying he was a current employee at the Carreras Universitarias de Belles Artes in Madrid and had been apprehended at his home where he appeared to be leaving to commit another rape. Such a small item had been on the front page with a bold headline; however, no picture of the rapist nor name had been released. The public was relieved at the news, and desirous of hearing how he had been apprehended, his criminal past, and all the gruesome details of his crimes. They were drawn to the malignancy of his evil works, like flies to a rotting piece of meat.

In less than fifteen minutes every seat in the courtroom was filled, every space along the back of the room was packed solid, and the hallway outside was also filled by those who had wished to be at the trial but hadn't gotten there quite soon enough. The noise of the spectators' conversations was so loud it

Chapter 31

seemed more like a sporting event rather than a serious trial that would decide the fate of the condemned. The press filled the front row of the courtroom, and they made a show of how many cameras they were going to use to document the proceedings.

As the prosecutor and his assistant entered and took their seats, the noise abated only insignificantly; but, as the defendant in handcuffs and his lawyer entered, everyone stopped talking and strained to get a glimpse at this horrible man who had kept all of Madrid on edge for such a long time. They were taken aback at his innocuous looks and demeanor. In front of them, "the monster" seemed to be a mild-mannered, professional-looking, tall and slender man with medium brown hair and brown eyes, who quietly sat beside his lawyer with a small smile. He didn't seem formidable at all.

They weren't sure what to make of the man they had all feared and now viewed. They weren't sure what they had expected to see, but this man didn't seem to come up to their expectations. As the audience was watching the accused rapist, the jurors were quickly brought in and seated in the jury box. They too, as soon as they were seated, perused the accused and wondered at his appearance.

As the judge entered, the bailiff asked all to stand and to be quiet, which they did. The judge took the bench, adjusted his glasses, rapped his gavel, and said loudly, "This courtroom is now in session."

Looking around the courtroom, he continued, "The country of Spain and the City of Madrid against the defendant, Professor-Señor Alejandro Villars Correao Castillo Bodega, for the crime of rape. You may be seated." Looking over to the defendant's table, he said, "Señor Villars, please stand."

The Urge

Villars looked at his lawyer and then slowly rose to his feet.

"Señor Villars, how do you plead, guilty or not guilty?"

Villars cleared his throat and responded. "Not guilty, Your Honor." His voice was so soft, and his answer was so polite that all present, including the judge, could scarcely believe their ears. The monster appeared to be a refined gentleman!

The judge said, "Your plea will be entered into the record" as he again struck his gavel.

The Bailiff said, "You may be seated."

Professor Villars sat down quietly beside his lawyer.

The judge then said, "I call the Prosecutor, Señor Victor Ventura to make his opening statement."

Prosecutor Ventura rose, walked to the jurors' box, and facing the jurors squarely stated, "The prosecution will assure this court that all our accumulated evidence will prove beyond a shadow of a doubt that Professor Villars is the serial rapist for whom Spanish authorities have been searching for the last twenty-five years."

At that figure, the entire courtroom attendees let out a huge gasp and many turned to their neighbors and started making comments. Within seconds the courtroom had again turned almost as noisy as before the trial had begun.

The judge banged his gavel loudly and said, "This courtroom will come to order at once." Directing his attention again to the prosecutor, he stated, "Please continue, Prosecutor Ventura."

"At this time, we will not be making any further statements, but we will let our evidence be released

Chapter 31

during the trial proceedings. It should be noted, however, that we will be revealing witnesses, DNA samples, photographs, and sworn testimonies that will convince the Jury of Professor Villars' guilt. We would ask the Jury to not only find him guilty of committing a number of rapes, but also to arrive at a proper punishment for his heinous deeds."

"Is that all?" Asked the judge.

"Yes, Your Honor." The prosecutor returned to his table.

The judge said, "Señor Contreras, would you please give your opening statement?"

Señor Contreras rose, slowly approached the Jury box, and said, "My client assures me there has been a horrible miscarriage of justice and he is not the man the authorities think he is. He has been wrongly arrested and accused.

"Señor Villars is a respected full professor of art at the Carreres Universitarias de Bellas Artes here in Madrid where he has been a faculty member for the last five years. Prior to that, he was an associate art professor in Barcelona. He has many students and colleagues who will testify to his upstanding citizenship, teaching abilities, and the love of his students, and fellowmen of all ages. We will prove that such an outstanding person could in no way be the serial rapist who the prosecution will try to prove he is. We ask that the Jury find him not guilty and will acquit him of all charges."

Señor Contreras smiled at the Jurors, then smiled at his client, then walked slowly back to the defendant's table and sat down.

"Thank you, gentlemen," the judge exclaimed. He directed his attention to the prosecutor, "Señor Ventura, please call your first witness."

The Urge

Prosecutor Ventura rose and said, "I call to the witness stand Police Detective Marielena Cortez-Rivera."

Sitting in the back of the courtroom where Professor Villars hadn't seen her, Marielena rose and came forward to the witness stand. Villars couldn't believe his eyes. Marielena was dressed in a police uniform and looked quite threatening. Not at all like he had previously known her. While he had discovered after she had taught in his classroom that she was an officer of the law, he really had not visualized her as anything but an artist. Now here she was, the first witness against him. As she reached the witness stand, his eyes roamed around the courtroom. He recognized several of the women who had been his rape victims, but he knew they couldn't recognize him. Thank God, he'd always worn a mask.

The judge swore in Marielena and, after she was sworn in, looked expectantly at Señor Ventura.

Señor Ventura asked, "Detective Cortez-Rivera, do you know the defendant?"

"Yes, sir. I do."

"Could you explain to the court how you became acquainted with Señor Villars?"

"Professor Villars contacted me shortly after I had completed a mural for the San Anton City Hall. He saw my picture and read the newspaper account of the mural dedication and how I also have one of my paintings in the Prado Museum. He arranged with his university that I come to speak at his art classes as a guest lecturer and demonstrator for a week."

"You have two jobs, an artist and a police detective?"

"Yes, that is correct."

Chapter 31

"Did he know you were a police detective?"

"Not to my knowledge. That fact wasn't mentioned in any publicity concerning my artworks."

"When you met Señor Villars, what was your impression of him?"

"I thought he was a very caring art professor who loved his students and wanted them to succeed. He was well-spoken and polite. He seemed a perfect gentleman."

"Was there anything which may have triggered your mind to think he might be a rapist?"

"Not at the time we first met."

"Was there anything about your sojourn at the university in Madrid that alerted you to a rapist?"

"I knew about the rapist prior to my being at the university. In my work as a police officer, our police department was well-informed that a rapist was at work in the Madrid area."

"But, what about when you were actually demonstrating and lecturing at the university?"

"Three days into my week working with his students Professor Villars told me that the students wanted to throw a celebration party for me at a local bar on the last night before I left for home. He explained that they were really appreciative of all the information which I had shared with them and thought it would be a way they could pay me back. He said that he, unfortunately, had previously made plans for that evening, but he would be there for at least part of the evening."

"And did he do that?"

"Yes, but he left quite early. Well before dark.

The Urge

I stayed at the party until I felt the students were starting to wander off into their own groups and after I had eaten. I was leaving Madrid the next morning for home." Marielena paused and looked directly at Professor Villars.

"Please continue," urged Señor Ventura.

"As I left the bar, I remembered what my self-defense mentor had said about walking streets alone after dark. I placed my car keys in my right hand with the sharp edges outward, and I put my purse in a cross-body carry."

"Did you have a car to match the car keys?"

"No. My car was at home. I had taken a train to Madrid and expected to return home the same way the next morning."

"Would you please explain the car keys then?"

"Master Chow, my self-defense instructor, had said that holding car keys in such a way enables a person to have a means of protecting themselves. It is especially good for women to do it."

"Did you feel safer?"

"Yes. I did feel strange, but since I had been working with the Madrid police force in the search of the serial rapist and being in Madrid myself, I did feel safer that way.'"

"So, you knew self-defense, and were well aware of the Madrid rapes, right?"

"Yes. My husband, Commissioner Rivera, of the San Anton police force, had insisted that I have an additional self-defense course with Master Chow. He knew that I am sometimes out alone doing my artwork. He was concerned with the number of rape

Chapter 31

cases being reported, as was I."

"Was there any other reason he was concerned?"

"Yes. I had been compiling a list of these rape cases. I had interviewed a number of victims and had arrived at a list of physical attributes of these victims. Because all the rapes were so similar and all of the victims were petite, under one-and-a-half meters in height and under or approximately forty kilos, my husband alerted me that my physical measurements were the same as the rapist's chosen victims."

"You were not only aware of the victims, but also their physical appearance?"

"That is correct."

"Let's return to where you left off. After you left the bar, did anything happen?"

"As I walked about a block from my hotel, I was attacked where the streetlights were non-existent and very dark."

"Please tell us exactly what happened."

"I fought back, using the skills which Master Chow had taught me. I stepped in close to the attacker, brought my right hand with the keys upward, and struck my attacker in the face, pulling downward with all my might."

"Did you connect with his face?"

"Yes."

"Did he say or do anything?"

"He didn't make a sound. He didn't say anything, but he swung me around. I hit a signpost and broke my left arm."

"Then what?"

The Urge

"I kicked him in the groin, and he doubled over. Then I turned quickly and gave him a roundhouse kick to his head. When he went down, I ran to my hotel and we, the desk clerk and I, called the police."

"Did they investigate?"

"They returned to the spot of the attack but found no one there."

"Was that the end of it?"

"Not really. As I tried to remember what happened, I thought the attacker looked somewhat familiar, but I couldn't think who he looked like. Then, the more other victims spoke to me during my investigation, almost all of them had also thought their attacker looked familiar."

"Was their description the same as yours? Was it Señor Villars?"

"Yes and no. All the descriptions led me to do a sketch of the rapist. Fortunately, I'm an artist too. It was not Professor Villars, but all the victims agreed with my sketch."

"Did you finally determine who the person was?"

"Yes. My husband and I were watching a documentary about Francisco Franco. I realized the sketch of the rapist which I had been working on of the rapist matched Francisco Franco. When I presented a photograph of Franco to all the victims, they also identified Franco. Because he was dead, no one, including myself, had made the connection."

"Did you make any other discoveries?"

"I surmised that the reason my attacker made no sound when I keyed his face during my attack, was because I hadn't hurt his face. I had torn a mask - a

Chapter 31

mask of Franco."

"Detective Cortez-Rivera, in doing your research to find the rapist, approximately how many rape victims have you interviewed?"

"Over thirty."

The courtroom was filled with gasps of amazement at the number of rapes that had been committed.

"Did all these victims describe their rapist resembling Francisco Franco?"

"All of them who had a chance to see their rapist's face, but one."

Turning to the prosecutor, the judge asked, "Señor Ventura, will we be hearing from all of these witnesses?"

"No, Your Honor. Only the most significant ones. I do, however, wish to offer as evidence the following list of the women who have all identified either the sketch or the photograph of Francisco Franco as their assailant. It also has the date and place of their attack."

"So accepted." The judge said., "Please continue your questioning of this witness."

Prosecutor Ventura turned to Marielena and asked, "I believe that you stated that you have a number of women who thought they recognized their attacker, who saw him. All but one identified the man as Francisco Franco either from your sketch or from a photo, is that correct?"

"Yes, sir. That is correct."

"Didn't you find that strange? They would recognize a dead man?"

"Not when the idea of a disguising mask was added. Many of the women had testified that their rapist's

The Urge

eyes looked strange or deeply sunken, which could be explained by someone wearing a mask. Your eyes never look exactly life-like when a full-face mask is worn. A mask also helped to explain how the rapist could avoid being caught for a long time."

"Let's go back for a moment. You said you'd interviewed over thirty women. Were they all from the Madrid area where rapes have been occurring during the last five years?"

"No, the were not. I interviewed women from Salamanca, Barcelona, Guadalajara, Toledo, Sevilla, and elsewhere."

With that response, the courtroom again buzzed like a hornet's nest.

The judge banged his gavel and again demanded that there be order.

Prosecutor Ventura never skipped a beat in his interrogation and asked, "All these women identified the attacker as Franco?"

"Of those who had a chance to see their attacker's face."

"All but one?"

"Now if the victims all identified a man who we know to be dead and who didn't look like the defendant, how did you link the defendant, Professor Villars, to a Franco mask?"

"That's a little complicated and took a lot of work. Because all of the rapes were so similar, it seemed to me as if he were in a play, replicating a scene over and over again with only the victim changing.

"I thought the rapist may have some acting experience, either professional or amateur. I wondered

Chapter 31

when in his lifetime he had been on stage. I could trace the rapes backward from Madrid to Barcelona; Barcelona to Bilbao, and Bilbao to San Sebastian.

"I knew by the dates, that whoever the rapist was had to have aged during that time. In going backward, he was getting younger and younger.

"There had been a rape in the Bilbao region where the victim had given a very good description of her assailant, and that description matched the descriptions of victims who identified the sketch or photo of Franco.

"Furthermore, the M.O. of the rape exactly matched the case I was working on. It was an old unsolved case that had haunted one of their detectives for years. Speaking to him and telling him of my mask theory and my idea that the rapist might have had some theatrical background, he remembered a play in Gernika where one of the actors played Franco and wore a Franco mask."

"Did that tie you to Professor Villars?"

"Not at first. There had been a fire in that theater that had burned their playbills and records, about a year or so after the production which I just mentioned. The current manager of this same theater had been a teenager when that play took place. He couldn't remember the actor's name but said if he ever saw him or a picture of him, he would recognize him. As a youngster, he was in awe of the actor's abilities - sort of hero worship."

"Were you able to produce a photo that he recognized?"

"Only later."

"How did you do it?"

The Urge

"We digitally manipulated a photo of Professor Villars as a young man."

Señor Contreras rose and shouted, "This is a figment of her imagination. It is all a contrived scheme to prosecute the defendant. I've listened patiently up to this point, but this testimony is ludicrous! I protest!"

The judge said, "Please resume your seat. I want to see where this line of questioning leads. Please continue Prosecutor Ventura."

Prosecutor Ventura asked, "Did you actually use a photo of Professor Villars?"

"Not at first, we first used other photos we had, in fact, a whole series of photos, which showed him at different ages."

Villars sat stunned. His thoughts were racing. How could they have found out about his earlier rapes and tied them all together? How far back had she gone in her search?

Turning to the judge, Prosecutor Ventura said, "Your Honor, I reserve the right to recall this witness anytime, but the evening is almost upon us. I ask for a recess until tomorrow morning."

The judge said, "I agree, the hour is late. We will resume the cross-examination of this witness by the defense tomorrow morning. This courtroom is adjourned until ten o'clock tomorrow." He then rapped his gavel and the courtroom emptied.

As the room cleared Señor Contreras looked at Professor Villars and said, "You were arrested with a Franco mask in your possession. How could that be?"

"I told you. I bought it for my mother's birthday. She still loves Franco. Besides, if the mask of the rapist was destroyed, supposedly by this witness

Chapter 31

and her keys during her attack, how could I have a Franco mask during my arrest except for the reason I've given. It's all circumstantial. I'm not the rapist. It's happenstance. She said it was not me who she recognized that attacked her. It had to be someone wearing a Franco mask, a different Franco mask than the one she talked about in that play."

~ ~

Chapter 32
Why

Damn Franco! Damn that Franco mask! Why had he ever decided to wear ANY mask, much less a FRANCO mask?

Even though he asked himself these questions, he knew the answers.

After he had committed his first rape, he realized that, if the girls or women whom he raped could identify him, he would be caught and incarcerated. He couldn't allow that to happen. Even though he hadn't committed many rapes while in high school, he still refused to have his face seen. He had purchased an inexpensive Halloween mask and used it during those couple of rapes. He had used the same mask when he went to college when he raped several women there. He had tried to limit "the urge" during his college years.

Like some of his college friends, he'd dated a few women and had sex with them. He had not used the mask with these women; since, after all, they knew

The Urge

him, and their coupling was consensual. But for the times when "the urge" was too strong and he'd felt the need to rape, he always used a mask. He knew what he was doing was wrong and he really didn't want to be found out.

He had always been interested in theater productions even in high school, but his school had been so small and what few productions had been put together amounted to very little - more as something to do and a way to entertain the community. When he had discovered the playhouse in Gernika, being an actor had been his true joy. There were so few good actors in that venue during that time and his acting skills were so far superior to everyone else's, he had been offered some really good roles in several productions. The roles had been challenging, and most satisfying to him. Most of all, they had given him a chance to hone his acting skills.

Because he was such a good actor, he reaped a good amount of acclaim. In one of the last plays, the chance to play Franco was his epitome of acting. His mother had absolutely adored Franco. Her descriptions to her son of Franco had made Franco seem almost godlike. To become Franco, even in a theater production, was almost perfect. It was the role in which he had truly come into his own.

Everyone, both in the cast and the audience, applauded so loudly for his portrayal that he could almost believe he had taken on the personality and power of Franco. He felt invincible. He felt he could do no wrong. He felt both dominant and dominating. It was a wonderful feeling. He truly was in control of himself and others. That role had seemed to give him everything he had missed his whole life. He had power, regard, respect, love, reverence, and glory. While he had played other roles in that playhouse, it

Chapter 32

was always the Franco role he remembered.

When that play was over and he continued raping women, he reverted to a mask of Franco. In his mind, he was Franco, and he could do anything he wanted. No one could touch him. He could have any woman he wanted. He could do with them as he wanted. He was almost superhuman.

He still wanted to cover his tracks though. Someone might associate him and his role as Franco, wearing a Franco mask in the play, with a Franco mask on a rapist. He couldn't allow that to happen.

As he was getting ready to graduate from college and take the job in Barcelona, he slipped into the theater one night through a window that he knew had a bad latch. With no one around, it had been easy to start a fire in the prop room which was right next to the office where all the old playbills and actors' files were located. He used a few of those playbills and some of the props, like a couple of old wooden swords and three oily pigment paint cans, to start the fire. With kindling and an accelerant, it hadn't taken much to get the blaze going.

He exited the building the same way he had entered. He stayed several blocks away in the shadows, watching the building become fully involved, and the firemen try to put it out. By the time he had left, both he and the firemen realized the building was a total loss as were its contents. He realized his past there was only a memory.

With his tracks very effectively covered, he had moved without a backward glance to Barcelona. No one would ever know. No one would ever place him as both the actor Franco and the rapist Franco.

Now here, in this courthouse years later, this same Franco mask was being used to pin him to his crimes.

The Urge

He couldn't let one mask, really two of the same kind put him away. He would continue to feign innocence. He would know nothing. Nothing.

He was totally exhausted. How many witnesses had seen that damn mask? How many witnesses had identified him?

After lying in his bed and trying to remember everything which had been said during the trial that day, another question popped into his mind. The topic of "other photographs" had been mentioned. How could they have photos of him?

In high school he'd used his Halloween mask, he'd even used it for a few rapes when he was in college. In college, he'd switched to the Franco mask. In Barcelona, he'd used the Franco mask. Since moving to Madrid, he'd used the Franco mask, whether in Madrid during weekday rapes or outside Madrid during the weekend rapes.

He had always used a mask, except once. No, that was so long ago, and he had been so young. No one could identify him now with that. He was now middle-aged. Preposterous! Why was he worried? He really didn't know. It was absolutely ludicrous that this artist/detective was after him. He'd been so good to her - and he really hadn't raped her. What did she have against him? She and the prosecution were making up evidence. It wouldn't work.

He rolled over, covered himself with his blanket, and tried to go to sleep. Day two of his trial was tomorrow. He'd get some sleep and look fresh and unconcerned tomorrow, not worn out and haggard. He'd put on a confident and unworried expression. He was innocent. After today's testimony, he truly believed they didn't have as much against him as he had feared.

~ ~

Chapter 33
Day 2 of the Trial

As the door of the courtroom opened, people rushed to fill every seat. The events revealed by the previous day's trial had been either read in the newspaper, heard on the local news stations, or been told person to person all over Spain. Many wondered how the defense would try to tear apart the star witness for the prosecution.

Again, the courtroom's noise level rose as the defendant was brought into the courtroom. How could this seemingly mild-mannered man be guilty of such evil? It didn't seem possible.

The jurors were ushered into the room and filled the jury box. The prosecution entered, the defendant and his attorney filed in, the bailiff had everyone stand, and then the judge took the bench. Finally, everyone was in their place. The judge banged his gavel loudly and called the court to order, telling all to sit.

The judge then turned to the prosecution and asked, "Do you wish to continue with the witness?"

The Urge

"Not at this time, Your Honor. I will wish to further question her later, however. I yield to the defense for cross-examination."

The judge turned to the defendant's table, looked at Señor Contreras, and asked, "Señor Contreras, do you wish to cross-examine Detective Cortez-Rivera?"

Señor Contreras rose and stated, "Yes, I do, Your Honor."

The judge said, "Detective Cortez-Rivera, please resume your seat in the Witness Stand. Remember that you are still under oath."

"Yes, Your Honor," said Marielena as she took her seat.

Señor Contreras walked over to her and asked, "Yesterday you said you used other pictures other than ones of Professor Villars to have the rape victims identify Professor Villars. I'm confused. Where were these other photos found? Who are these photos of? How would photos of someone else point to Professor Villars? Do you really want us to believe all this nonsense?"

Marielena took a deep breath, looked over at Professor Villars, and then at Prosecutor Ventura, who slightly nodded his head, looked down, and smiled. She then looked directly at Señor Contreras and said in a firm voice, "Pictures of his son."

Señor Contreras exclaimed, "His son?"

"Yes. That was the one rape he will never be able to deny. The one where the victim recognized Professor Villars for who he really is, or should I say was; because it occurred when he was a teenager."

"What?" Yelled Professor Villars, jumping to his feet.

Chapter 33

The judge then said, "Señor Contreras, will you please control your client? Professor Villars, take your seat and be quiet."

Professor Villars slowly sat down. The shock was too much. A son? Who? Where? How had that happened? No? It couldn't be.

The courtroom again filled with chaotic voices. The judge asked both Prosecutor Ventura and Señor Contreras to approach the bench. Lowering his voice, he asked the prosecutor if he knew the last information to which Señor Ventura nodded in the affirmative. The judge directed his attention to Señor Contreras. He told him that he must keep his client in check. He also asked him if he had known about a son.

Señor Contreras replied, "I received that information only this morning from the Prosecution; and, when I asked my client if he had any children, he swore to me that he did not."

The judge then directed both attorneys to resume their positions. Banging his gavel he said, "This trial will continue; and I wish to remind all spectators that if they cannot remain silent, I will clear the courtroom of all persons except those that are necessary."

Señor Contreras walked over to his client, looked down, and quietly asked again if he had known that he had a son, to which Villars said, "No."

Then the defense attorney turned to Marielena and loudly stated, "My client has just informed me again that he has no son. Please explain your comment concerning photos of his son. What evidence do you have for that statement?"

Marielena glanced at the prosecutor and nodded as she said, "In our investigation into a rape in Irun, Professor Villars, at the time a teenager, raped a young

The Urge

girl in a park who became pregnant with a son. We're not sure if Villars ever knew he had a son. Now he does because we can prove it."

Señor Contreras was so surprised he stammered, "I have no further questions for this witness at this time. I need to consult with my client again on this matter."

The judge directed his attention to Prosecutor Ventura and asked, "Do you wish to continue with Detective Cortez-Rivera?"

"Not at this time. Instead, I would like to call to the stand Señorita Helena Diez Urbi de Leon Silva. From the back of the courtroom came a very small woman who walked slowly up to the witness box. She stepped up into the Witness Box and settled herself in the chair.

Professor Villars swore to himself that he had never seen her before in his entire lifetime. As she had walked down to the witness box, however, he had glimpsed a young man who had been sitting with her and who had moved aside to let her out of her seat. He didn't believe his eyes. It was as though he was looking in a mirror at himself as a younger man. But the hair, the eyes, and the complexion were all wrong. No. It couldn't be!

Señorita Diez looked around at the courtroom and then over at Professor Villars almost as if she were in a daze.

Prosecutor Ventura patted her hand and smiled at her as he asked, "Are you comfortable?"

"Yes," she responded.

"Good. Now, if you could please tell the Jury about your experience with the defendant. You were a young girl at the time, I understand, so take your time and leave nothing out."

Chapter 33

She paused before speaking, and then deliberately speaking clearly, she said, "He raped me."

Everyone in the courtroom drew a quick breath.

She continued, "It was years ago, and he was a teenager and so was I. I had broken up with my boyfriend and I was crying. I walked into a playground. There he was. He tried to comfort me, but he ended up taking advantage of me. I never saw him again until today. But this isn't the first time I've laid eyes on him since that evening. Every day I've seen him. The son that I conceived from that rape looks exactly like him. Therefore, for years, I've had to see him again and again and again." At that, she sobbed and reached into her pocket for a handkerchief to wipe her eyes.

Prosecutor Contreras asked, "Obviously, your rapist wasn't wearing a Franco mask, was he?"

"No. I saw his real face."

"And do you recognize this person, this 'he' whom you refer to as your rapist?"

"Yes. He's sitting right there." She pointed at Professor Villars. "He's the defendant, Professor Villars."

"You said your son looks just like him?"

"Yes."

"Is your son here in the courtroom with you today?"

Tears streamed down Señorita Diez's face as she said softly, "Yes."

"I have no further questions at this time for this witness," said Prosecutor Ventura.

The judge turned to Señor Contreras and asked, "Do you wish to cross-examine?"

The Urge

"Yes, I certainly do!" Striding to the witness box he said, "Who put you up to this charade?"

"What charade?" Asked Señorita Diez. "This is no charade. My son and I both consented to a DNA examination that was matched to the DNA sample of Professor Villars. My Henri is the professor's son."

Señor Contreras stomped back to the defendant's table. "I'm finished with this witness. This whole trial is becoming a dog and pony show."

The judge said, "Señor Contreras, please compose yourself." Turning to the witness box, he said, "Señorita Diez, you are excused." She slowly exited the box and walked to the back of the courtroom. After she had cleared the aisle, the judge said, "Prosecutor Ventura, please call your next witness."

Prosecutor Ventura said, "I call Señor Henri Diez Urbi de Leon Silva to the Witness Stand."

Henri rose beside his mother and strode up the aisle that she had just vacated. He took the stand and was sworn in.

Prosecutor Ventura asked him, "How old are you?"

"Twenty-five years old."

"You are the result of your mother being raped by Villars?"

"Yes. The DNA results confirmed it."

"Why did you consent to be a witness against your father?"

"I do not consider him my father. He was only a sperm donor who wrecked my mother's and my life. I consented to be a witness because I want to see Villars pay for his crimes. If I had a father, a real father, he would have been a loving man who would have taken

Chapter 33

care of a loving woman like my mother and who would have made sure she didn't suffer the societal brutality all these years for an incident which wasn't her fault. She was a victim of this man. Unfortunately, I look like him, so she has had to suffer doubly every time she looked at me - a son whom she raised by herself and has been humiliated for. I was told the statute of limitations for her has expired, but all the women he has raped throughout the years have suffered at his hands through no fault of theirs. I wanted to testify to bring awareness that rape is not the woman's fault but the rapist's fault."

"Thank you, Señor Diez. That is all I have to ask you."

The judge said, "You're excused - unless, Señor Contreras has any cross-examination?"

Señor Contreras, looking like a shell-shocked soldier, said softly, "No, Your Honor. I have no questions for this witness."

The judge looked at his watch. "Because of the hour, I am going to postpone any further witnesses until tomorrow. Señor Contreras, I think you need to consult with your client. Prosecutor Ventura, do you have more witnesses to question?"

"Yes, Your Honor. Several more witnesses and I will recall Detective Cortez-Rivera again to the stand."

"How many days do you anticipate these witnesses will take?"

"Probably at least two prior to the defense's case."

"Thank you. This court is now adjourned until ten o'clock tomorrow. Bailiff clear the courtroom."

As Señor Contreras looked at Professor Villars, he said, "I knew you were guilty, but I had no idea you've

The Urge

been raping women for twenty-five years. There is no way I'm going to be able to get you out of this. You're going to have to change your plea and hope for some kind of leniency."

"Never!" Said Villars.

~ ~

Chapter 34
Day 3 of the Trial

    Marielena, Diego, the Prosecutor, and the Madrid detectives met two hours prior to the courtroom opening on the third day. They knew that this was going to be another strong day for them. They had arranged for the forensic computer specialist; the Madrid and the Seville witnesses, both of whom had DNA evidence to prove Villars' guilt; the sworn statement from the storekeeper where Villars had purchased the new mask, and the sworn statement from the theater manager in Gernika to be introduced today. Marielena knew she would also be on the witness stand again, this time to clarify how they had traced the mask purchase as well as the software program used to get their identifying photographs. Everything was ready, but everything had to be introduced in the proper order for the maximum effect on the Jurors. They were glad the Jurors were being sequestered for the entire week because they felt they needed that much time to be sure the Jury would not only vote Villars guilty but also impose the maximum penalty for his crimes.

The Urge

If the defense attorney needed more than this week to present his side, they knew the judge could extend the Jury sequestering time.

They walked as a group to the courtroom just as the doors were opening. The rush of spectators almost ran over them as the public was drawn to the trial like a magnet by all the gruesome details which had already been revealed. The thirst for every little dirty nuance surrounding the monster was insatiable. They watched as the Jurors were ushered into the Jury Box and observed that their two first witnesses were present.

Finally, Professor Villars entered with his court-appointed lawyer, Señor Contreras. Both seemed even quieter than they had the previous two days. They never even looked at each other.

The bailiff asked that all stand as the judge entered. As the judge took the bench, he perused the courtroom and realized there was not one square centimeter of the room that was not filled. He sighed as he realized this was to be another day the prosecution would hammer more nails in Villars's coffin. But, so be it. It wasn't as though he didn't deserve it from the evidence which had already been presented. He wondered to himself why Villars hadn't changed his plea. What did he and his defense attorney have up their sleeves that could possibly prove his innocence? Or - was it all bravado? Did they think there was some technicality they could exploit? Did they think they could bluff their way out of the surmounting evidence being presented? He'd have to be really careful to make sure justice was served, that he made no mistake that could turn things around, and that he, at least tried to give them a chance to present some sort of defense.

After a few seconds, he said, "This court now comes

Chapter 34

to order. Prosecutor Ventura, please present your first witness."

Prosecutor Ventura rose and said, "I call Señor Eduardo Escobar to the witness stand."

A slim young man rose and walked to the witness stand. Villars couldn't understand what was going on and whispered to his attorney, "Who is he?" Señor Contreras held his finger to his lips to silence him.

After Señor Escobar was sworn in, Prosecutor Ventura asked him, "Señor Escobar, what is your profession?"

"I am a forensic computer specialist."

"What is your connection to this trial?"

"I am the person responsible for the series of photographs which were digitally manipulated of Henri Diez."

"Have you ever been asked to do a series of such photographs in other criminal cases?"

"Yes, Sir."

"Have those other photographs ever been altered in any way other than to change the age of the person?"

"Not usually, but sometimes hair or eye color is sometimes enhanced. With the technology which is available now, not just to police departments, but to anyone who is computer-literate, changing the age of a person without changing anything else is very easy; and, adding a different eye or skin or hair color is no problem."

"On the series of photographs of Henri Diez, did you make such changes?"

"Yes. Henri's mother stated to the police officers

The Urge

involved that Henri looked just like his father, except for his hair, eye, and skin colors. When I changed those, she identified his father, Professor Villars. Then I made a series of photos at different ages."

"So - this is a common manipulation for a computer expert, such as yourself?"

"Yes, Sir."

"I have no further questions for this witness, Your Honor," said Señor Ventura.

The judge turned to Señor Contreras and asked, "Do you wish to cross-examine this witness?"

"Yes, Your Honor."

Señor Contreras adjusted his glasses, and, looking directly at Señor Escobar, asked, "How much did the Prosecution pay you to change the photos?"

The courtroom erupted in loud voices.

The judge banged his gavel and shouted, "This courtroom will come to order. And, Señor Contreras, please approach the bench."

Señor Contreras walked up to the judge's bench and the judge said, "That question was totally out of line. Please be careful that you do not accuse any member of our police force of such disregard of the law again, or I will personally find you in contempt of the court and slap liable charges on you." Turning to the jury, he continued by saying, "You will disregard the last question to this witness. Señor Contreras, do you have any further questions for this witness?"

"No, your Honor."

"Then please take your seat. Señor Ventura, please call your next witness."

Chapter 34

"I call Maria Alvelar Clarita Cases Jerez to the witness stand."

A very small young woman walked to the witness stand, was sworn in, and nervously looked over at Professor Villars at the defense table.

Prosecutor Ventura cleared his throat loudly, drawing attention to himself as if the entire courtroom hadn't avidly been watching him and this new witness. Clearing his throat, a second time, he said, "Señorita Alvelar, I understand you have been a rape victim. Could you please describe the situation of that rape to the Jury?"

"Yes, sir. I and my best friend had shopped that afternoon. We went to dinner, to a tapas bar, and to a nightclub where we danced. Her boyfriend met us at the bar and spent the evening escorting us from place to place."

Señor Contreras yelled, "Do we need to know all these details? Get to it, if you can!"

The spectators started to laugh.

The judge said, "Please Señor, be patient. AND QUIET! I just warned you about your behavior."

Prosecutor Ventura said encouragingly, "Please continue, Señorita Alvelar."

"After midnight they went home."

Please define for us the word 'they'?"

"My girlfriend and her boyfriend. They left me when I was three blocks from my apartment. I thought three blocks would be fine. I knew about the serial rapist in the Madrid area, but I didn't believe he'd be in my neighborhood."

"Please continue."

The Urge

"As I walked past an underground parking garage, I was grabbed from behind." She paused and tears trickled down her cheeks.

"Take your time. It's OK. Tell us what happened then."

"The man told me not to scream and he wouldn't hurt me. He then stuffed something in my mouth so I couldn't scream. I could barely breathe. He dragged me down into the garage, pushed me down, and raped me."

"Did you know him? Did you recognize him?"

"I had a good look at him, but I didn't know him at that time."

"Later?"

"Later Detective Cortez-Rivera showed me both a sketch and a photograph that I did recognize him."

"What was your recognition?"

"The rapist was Franco, which made no sense to me. Franco is long dead and buried."

"Was there anything about the rape that could lead us to the defendant?"

"Yes. I reported the rape to the police immediately. They had me come into the hospital - which I did. As I was examined, pubic hair, not my own was found. It was assumed by the medical technician and the police that the pubic hair belonged to the rapist."

"Was anything ever done about the pubic hair?"

"Yes. They were used to get a DNA sample of the rapist."

"Do you know if anyone was linked to that DNA?"

Chapter 34

"Yes. I understand that the pubic hair DNA was matched to the DNA of Professor Villars, and the pubic hair itself was a match to Villars's pubic hair."

A gasp went through the courtroom.

Prosecutor Ventura asked, "Is there anything else you'd like to tell us about the rapist at this time?"

"No, not really; but the rapist was soft-spoken and polite."

Prosecutor Ventura said, "I have nothing further for this witness."

The judge turned to Señor Contreras and asked, "Do you wish to cross-examine?"

Señor Contreras stood, approached the witness box, and asked, "Señorita Alvelar, are you a DNA expert?"

"No. I really don't know anything about DNA except what I learned in school."

"And - you're willing to believe that pubic hair is enough to lead you to accuse Professor Villars of being your rapist? Are you that naive?"

"Sir, with all due respect. I didn't analyze it. The real experts did. If they say there's a match between Professor Villars' DNA and pubic hair found on me, I believe them. They do - and I do believe he is the one who raped me."

"I have no further questions."

The judge said, "You're excused."

As she left the witness stand, the judge turned to Prosecutor Ventura and said, "Please call your next witness."

Prosecutor Ventura said, "I call Marisol Huevos

The Urge

Juarez Rios Ramerez to the witness stand."

As with all the other women who had testified before, including Detective Cortez-Rivera, a petite young woman rose from her seat and walked forward to the witness stand where she was sworn in.

"Señorita Huevos, do you live in Madrid?"

"No. My home is in Seville," she said softly.

The spectators in the courtroom strained to hear her words as did the judge and Prosecutor.

"Señorita Huevos, could you please repeat that louder?"

"Yes, sir. My home is in Seville, not Madrid."

"Did you know there was a serial rapist in the Madrid area?"

"Yes, it was in the news reports on the television; but Madrid is Madrid, and Seville is Seville. The two are quite a distance from each other so I wasn't worried."

"So - you assumed, did you not, that you were safe being in Seville?"

"Yes, I did."

"Please describe in detail the night you were raped."

"I had been drinking with my boyfriend. We got into an argument, and he stormed out of the bar leaving me all alone. I also left the bar, and I wandered along the riverfront feeling sorry for myself. It wasn't the first time we'd argued. He had a tendency to drink too much and become verbally abusive. I was trying to tell myself I'd be better off without him. But - it still hurt."

"Are you still with him?"

"No. That night I'd just come to a decision not to see

Chapter 34

him anymore and was about to return to my apartment when I was attacked in a very dimly lit and quite shady part of the Riverwalk. The man grabbed me, stuffed something in my mouth so I couldn't scream, ripped away my undergarments, and raped me."

"Then what happened?"

"Even though he had told me not to fight, I was already angry at my boyfriend and was further enraged by this creep who attacked me. I lost control and fought as hard as I could. He hit me and drug me into the shadows, but I could feel the skin on his arm. I have very long fingernails, so I dug into his arm. I must have hurt him because he knocked me out. When I awoke, he was gone. I found a policeman several blocks away and reported the rape. He immediately took me for a physical examination. That's when the technician found the blood and skin cells of the rapist under my fingernails. He also confirmed that I had been raped by my attacker when I was unconscious."

"Do you know what was done with those cells?"

"Yes, sir. They took and analyzed them for DNA."

"What was the result?"

"The DNA of my rapist matched the DNA sample of Professor Villars."

"This has been confirmed?"

"Yes. This is what the authorities told me."

"Did you get a good look at your attacker at the time of the rape?"

"Not a good look, but enough to recognize that it was the same person whose sketch Detective Cortez-Rivera showed me that was done from the descriptions by all his other victims."

The Urge

"Thank you, I have no further questions."

The judge then said, "Señor Contreras, do you wish to cross-examine?"

"Yes, Your Honor, I do," said Señor Contreras as he stood and walked to the Witness Box. Looking up at Señorita Huevos he asked, "You said the area of the park where you were attacked was, I believe you said, dimly lit. Was it dark?"

"No, not dark; there was some light, so I'd say the light there was dim."

"You weren't able to see your attacker's face, were you?"

"I could see his face. I was quite close to him as we struggled. Close enough to have scratched his forearm. Therefore, I did see his face."

"What did he look like?"

"Strange, but quite recognizable. Mustache, receding hairline, short brownish hair. The eyes were deeply set and didn't seem real. I was told after I identified the sketch that I'd seen a mask of Franco. Detective Cortez-Rivera also showed me a photo of Franco, so I indeed recognized my attacker."

"Do you believe your rapist wore a Franco mask?"

"Yes, sir, I do."

"Thank you. I have no further questions."

The judge then said, "Señorita Huevos, you're excused. Prosecutor Ventura, please call your next witness." Prosecutor Ventura said, "I wish to recall Detective Cortez-Rivera to the stand."

Marielena walked up the aisle and again took a seat in the witness stand.

Chapter 34

Prosecutor Ventura reminded her that she was still under oath and asked, "Detective Cortez-Rivera, could you please enlighten us again about the Franco masks?"

"As I mentioned previously when I was attacked, I realized the rapist not only wore a mask but that I had damaged it with my car keys. As I helped the Madrid police gather data and testimonies from the rapes after my attack, the most recent victims continued to identify their attacker as looking like Franco. They identified him with both my sketch of the rapist and with the Franco photograph. I then surmised that the rapist had acquired another Franco mask, a new one. Commissioner Rivera and I, with the help of the Madrid police force, made a list of every possible source that one might turn to in acquiring a new mask of Franco."

"Did you have any success in your search for that source?"

"Yes. I have here the result of that search - a sworn testimony of the salesman who sold Professor Villars his new Franco mask."

Prosecutor Ventura took the paper from Marielena, handed it to the judge, and said, "We present this notarized testimony to be used as evidence against Professor Villars." Then, turning back to Marielena, he said, "Can you tell the jury what is included in this testimony?"

"The testimony says that Professor Villars came into the store and purchased a Franco mask. It also says that when shown a photo of Professor Villars, the salesman positively identified him as the purchaser."

"We understand from the Madrid police that Professor Villars, the owner of a Franco mask, had it in his possession when he was apprehended. Is that

The Urge

correct?"

"Yes, that's correct."

Turning to the judge, he said, "The Prosecution will allow cross-examination of this witness before proceeding, You Honor."

The judge said to Señor Contreras, "Please proceed with your cross-examination."

Señor Contreras walked slowly to the witness box, as if in deep thought. Meanwhile, Villars laughed to himself. *This is where we show our artist/cop is a liar. I already covered my tracks with that salesman and the arresting officers about my buying the mask for my mother's birthday party. If we can prove this "artist/cop" is lying, we might put her whole story in doubt.*

Señor Contreras cocked his head slightly and asked, "Detective Cortez-Rivera, did you or anyone have a chance to talk to this salesman?"

"Yes, sir. My husband, Commissioner Rivera spoke at length with him."

"What did Professor Villars say to this salesman at the time of purchase?"

"He said that he was buying it for his mother's birthday party."

"But you didn't believe that. Why?"

"Several reasons, the first was I already knew Professor Villars, the rapist, had resumed his rapes using a new mask as a disguise from testimonies of new rapes. Second, Villars was arrested with it in his pocket along with a rag and a condom which fit the M.O. of our rapist. Third, if Professor Villars was on his way to his mother's birthday party, it seemed strange that he would also be carrying a condom. Fourth, his

Chapter 34

mother who lived in Biarritz in the upper part of our peninsula died three years ago. This must have been some sort of belated birthday party - after her death. She could never see that mask. We researched Villars's excuse after he was apprehended. He also used that same excuse about a birthday party with the arresting officers."

Señor Contreras's face look totally startled. He then looked over at his client and said, "He also told me the same reason for having the mask. I have no further questions for this witness." As he sat down at the defendant's table, he whispered to Villars, "Everything you've told me has been a lie. A preposterous lie."

The judge then said, "Prosecutor Ventura, do you have further questions for this witness?"

"Yes, Your Honor."

"Please proceed then."

"Detective Cortez-Rivera, could you please continue describing your timeline which you developed concerning any rapes which you believe have been the work of the defendant?"

"If we could have the screen dropped down and show the charts and corresponding map of Spain, please?"

The Prosecutor signaled to the court technician to project both the charts and the maps side-by-side on the screen.

Marielena continued, "A list of unsolved rape cases from several parts of Spain with the dates of their occurrences were compared with the dates and timelines of Professor Villars from his boyhood near San Sebastian, his college years near Bilbao, his associate professorship in Barcelona, and his current

The Urge

employment here in Madrid. As you can see, I've put the dates on the map of when Professor Villars lived in each place so you can trace his movement throughout Spain. If you compare the timetable of unsolved rapes, each series of rapes began and then ceased, whenever Professor Villars moved. The fact that the M.O. of all these cases was identical, which I know since I have traced down most of the victims to speak to them concludes that they were all conducted by one man, our defendant, Professor Villars."

Prosecutor Ventura then asked, "If Professor Villars has been at work for this many years, why hasn't he been suspected of them or apprehended before now?"

"Several reasons. First, he used a disguise. Second, he was careful. Third, his overall appearance and behavior really didn't seem fit with the public image of the heinous person he really is. Only a few people had a hunch he might be something other than he portrayed himself to be."

"Can you explain that please?"

"In researching the characteristics of serial rapists, the literature said that most are not actually identified or offered the psychological care they really need. Even as young people, many are not even suspected of having such evil characteristics. In Professor Villars' case, I spoke with his major college professor who told me that some of his artwork was bizarre enough that several faculty members thought he might have some kind of psychological problem. When one questioned him and tried to get him into counseling, Villars laughed him off saying he was fine. There was nothing wrong with him that needed counseling; he just saw the world differently, so his art was unique."

"Did his professors insist on counseling?"

Chapter 34

"No. They let it drop. At that time abstract art was all the rage, so they took his word at it that there was nothing wrong with him."

Prosecutor Ventura said, "I have no further questions at this time."

The judge asked, "Señor Contreras, do you wish to cross-examine?"

Señor Contreras rose and asked Marielena, "You yourself are an artist?"

"Yes."

"Did you have a chance to see Professor Villars' artwork?"

"No."

"You can't testify as to the 'strange quality' of his art?"

"No."

"Thank you. That is all."

Prosecutor Ventura turned to the judge and said, "Your Honor, the hour is late. If it is possible, could we continue tomorrow?"

Looking at his watch, the judge said, "I think that would be appropriate at this time. This court is adjourned until ten o'clock tomorrow. Bailiff, clear the courtroom." He rapped his gavel.

~~

Chapter 35
The Judge

Judge Umberto Castellanos Arbolitos Morano Garcia had been appointed to try this case. He wished some other judge had been given the assignment, but assignments were distributed on a rotating system in the Madrid jurisdiction in the Spanish courts. He had been at the top of the list to receive the next trial. So be it - but he was well aware of the seriousness of this case. If he messed up not only would all the women in Spain be up in arms, but he knew he would not live down the notoriety it would cause him personally. He would be an anathema. He might not ever be given an important trial again to try. Worse than that, he would never forgive himself. He could make no mistakes. He had to be sure there would be no chance of a mistrial. From the information he had been supplied by the prosecution, it seemed to be a slam-dunk. Villars was quite obviously guilty. He had no doubt of that. But he had to be sure the defense had every opportunity to prove Villars' innocence. It was his job not to seem prejudiced in any way.

The Urge

At his age of sixty-three, he had only a few more years until he could choose to retire. His long career on the bench had started thirty years earlier when he had given up his private law practice. Prior to that time, he'd spent three years working for prosecution lawyers as a clerk and hour years for the state as a novice defense attorney. He'd seen both sides of the law before becoming a defense attorney for three years. When he had been approached by the state to become a judge, he had felt he was more than qualified to do a fair job.

In his thirty years as a judge, he had presided over murder trials, property dispute trials, divorce trials, child custody trials, and trials for theft, personal abuse, rape, and defamation. He had never presided over a *serial* rapist trial. Serial rape trials were few and far between. They were the cause of most women's worst nightmares. He himself thought all rapists should be killed, but Spain had no death sentence. If not death, then he believed perhaps life in prison was probably the best end to such trials. He wouldn't have to decide. This was a jury trial, and the jury would have to decide.

It would be up to him that the trial would proceed in an orderly and lawful progression to its conclusion. He was glad it was a jury trial since that would allow his personal prejudice not to show. His voice would not be the one to put this man away. He would only parrot the jury's decision for Villars' future.

So far, he felt the trial had proceeded in a very good direction. What he had been impressed with the most was Detective Marielena Cortex-Rivera, both as a detective and also as a witness. She had been attacked very hard by the defense attorney, Señor Contreras. She had never batted an eyelash. She had remained cool and collected under fire. Her evidence was damning; and, from his talk to the prosecution

Chapter 35

lawyer, Señor Ventura, she had practically solved this case all by herself. She knew she had been attacked by Villars and, easily could have been one of his rape victims. Most women would have been so angry they would have shown that anger on the witness stand. Detective Cortez-Rivera had displayed absolutely no anger in her testimony in the witness box. On the contrary, her testimony had been given in a quiet, unemotional, and professional manner. Detective Cortez-Rivera was quite a woman, and definitely an asset to any police force where she might be employed.

He was looking forward to tomorrow's testimony. What other evidence would the prosecution be able to add to their already overwhelming volume of data? On the contrary, what kind of defense would be presented by Señor Contreras? Did he expect to pull some kind of defense "rabbit out of his hat" to save Villars? It would have to be a huge rabbit at this point. His job would be to allow the defense to give their side and to prevent them from destroying the strong case that the prosecution had already presented. Fairness. It was such a simple word. But one never knew. He'd seen past trials ellipse in an opposite direction during latter trial days and criminals escape seemingly very clear prosecutions. On this he was sure, the courtroom would again be packed, the press would be writing about this trial for years, and he was right in the center. He really needed a good night's sleep to be ready for whatever might transpire. He wanted no big, bad surprises.

~ ~

Chapter 36
Day 4 of the Trial

Again, the Prosecutor, Diego, Marielena, and the Madrid police force met two hours prior to the opening of the courtroom. There were to be two witnesses against Villars today, the mother of the young victim from Toledo and the young office worker from Madrid. Both were to be brought into the courtroom after it was in session. The twelve-year-old girl was too young to be interrogated on the witness stand, but her parents had begged to have her mother testify as to the brutality of the attack. Everyone in their neighborhood had already known about the attack so there was nothing to hide. Everyone sympathized with the girl and her parents and wanted the rapist to be punished for the rape. The office worker had also begged to be a witness, because she wanted her boyfriend, who had finally come back to her, to see that she was only one victim of this fiendishly, horrible rapist and to prove it wasn't her fault.

As the group gathered, Marielena said to them, "I've been thinking during this last day about our unsolved

The Urge

rape cases. What is the possibility that Villars might have committed all of them? None of them have been solved and there are no other suspects. Could that be a possibility? I've also wondered about where these rapes occurred. Villars seemed to conduct his rapes in Madrid during the weekdays and elsewhere on the weekends. Would the unsolved rapes also fit into a pattern, just like the solved ones do?"

The group thought for a moment and then Lieutenant Mendoza said, "It's a possibility. I personally am haunted by a case we had of a university student here in Madrid who had not only been raped but was killed. She was found by her three roommates before we were called in to investigate. If I remember correctly, she had the same physical characteristics as Villars' other victims. That rape occurred during a weekday night. Her roommates said she was to have a test the next day which would have been a school day during the week. While we have no M.O. or any victim's testimony, it might be worth looking into. I think she'd fit into Villars's pattern and timetable."

"Could Villars be a murderer as well as a rapist? Serial rapists usually don't kill their victims, but he's proved he's strong enough. And - what if he lost his temper?" said Marielena. She paused to let that idea sink in.

Lieutenant Mendoza said, "That could be true. But in that particular case, he left no clues."

Marielena said, "That may not be true. Let's look at the dates when we know he committed rapes and see where the dates of unsolved rapes, particularly that one, fall. If we can see a frequency in his rape pattern and our unknown rapes fall in the gaps in his pattern, we may be able to convince the Jury that he committed them too, especially that one. It could lead

Chapter 36

to a possible murder charge on top of the rape charges he already faces." She paused again and said, "I wonder what would happen if we got him on the stand under oath - would he lie about that rape too?"

Detective Mendoza said, "Probably. He seems to be lying about everything else that we have on him. Let's also not forget that he is an accomplished actor."

Marielena said, "Let's run a quick computer analysis of all the rapes, both those which we know he's committed and our unsolved rapes, and see where those dates fall, at least the ones here in Madrid. Maybe we'll get lucky and the one with the murdered university student who was also raped, will fall in one of the gaps in his rape history?"

Diego said, "It's certainly worth a try. If your police department has a real computer expert that could do it quickly?" He stopped for a moment. "If we could present this information during the trial, even if we could better still, present it at the end of today's trial, it might shake him up enough that he'll reconsider and change his plea to guilty?"

Detective Mendoza grinned and said, "I know of just the woman. She hasn't been in our department long, but she has managed to put together facts for several cases which we had previously missed. Her name is Teresa Terrapiña."

"Could we call her in now, describe what we're looking for, and have her run a quick analysis?" asked Marielena.

The Prosecutor said, "It will have to be real quick because it's almost time for today's session to begin. In fact, the doors to the courtroom should be opening in ten minutes."

Detective Mendoza sprang to his feet and hurried

The Urge

out of the room. The rest also got to their feet and walked to the courtroom. The halls were packed with people waiting to enter. Unlike the previous day when they entered and the crowd had practically trampled them, they went down a back hallway and entered through the rear of the room before the doors were opened. They were happy of that decision as a real stampede of spectators occurred when the doors were opened.

Entering down the same hallway and door, the jurors were ushered into the courtroom. As the noise level rose while all the anxious observers found seats, spectators turned to their neighbors and began speculating about what would be revealed in today's session. The defense attorney, Señor Contreras, and the defendant, Professor Villars, were then brought in. A brief silence overtook the room as all strained to again see "the monster".

After a brief moment, the bailiff said, "All rise", as the judge emerged from his chambers and took the bench.

The judge, after adjusting his robes, looked around the room, rapped his gavel, and declared, "You may be seated, this court is now in session. Prosecutor Ventura, please call your first witness."

Prosecutor Ventura rose from his seat and said, "I call to the witness stand Señorita Louisa Rios Montaro Estreño Buho."

A petite woman walked up to the witness stand and was sworn in.

Prosecutor Ventura glanced at Professor Villars before saying, "Señorita Rios, could you please enlighten us about your experience several months ago?"

Chapter 36

"I work in the downtown business district of Madrid in a financial office. I had worked overtime, which wasn't unusual, but that evening I left work well after dark. My boyfriend had been warning me about leaving the office late because he was worried about the reports concerning a serial rapist. For some reason, I hadn't thought much about it, but as I entered the underground public parking garage to go to my car, a man came up to me asking if I could make change for him to pay his parking ticket. He seemed to stumble close to me, and I got a good look at his face. Even as I thought I should avoid him, he grabbed me and pulled me down between a parked car and a van. As he did so, he jabbed a rag in my mouth. I couldn't make a sound. He said very softly that if I didn't fight, he wouldn't hurt me. I guess I was in shock because I didn't fight. He raped me. I kept remembering the words of my boyfriend warning me against being alone and being the victim of a possible rapist. I was numb. I hadn't done anything to ask to be raped. I guess I was at the wrong place at the wrong time."

"What was the aftermath of your rape?"

"My boyfriend kept saying to me, 'I told you so, you wouldn't listen, and now you're damaged goods.'"

"Does he still feel that way?"

"No. Since this trial began, he has seen that any woman can be a rape victim. He has apologized and told me, 'Women are victims, not the cause of rapes.' We are now engaged to be married. He also said that he should have come after me and taken me home himself which he will do if I have to work late again."

Prosecutor Ventura asked, "Can you describe your rapist?"

"When I was shown Detective Cortez-Rivera's

The Urge

sketch and a photograph of Franco, I immediately recognized the rapist."

"You've heard Detective Cortex-Rivera's testimony about her attack and when it occurred?"

"Yes."

"Was your rape after her attack or before so we can get a sense of the rapist's timeline of rapes or attempted rapes?"

"It was before her attack."

"And, he was wearing a Franco mask?"

"Yes."

"Is there any doubt in your mind that your rapist is not the same rapist as the person who attacked Detective Cortez-Rivera and these other women who have testified?"

"No doubt at all. It has to be the same man."

"Thank you. I have no further questions."

The judge looked over at the defendant's table and asked, "Señor Contreras, do you wish to cross-examine?"

"Yes, Your Honor. I do." Standing and walking to the witness box, he asked, "Señorita Rios, you say you later recognized the photo and sketch of your assailant, is that not correct?"

"Yes, sir."

"Didn't Detective Cortez-Rivera say as she showed you the sketch and photo of Franco that here was a sketch and photo of the person they knew was committing rapes in the Madrid area?"

"No, sir. She showed me a number of photos and

Chapter 36

asked me if I could identify my attacker? Only later, after I had identified a photo of Franco, did she show me the sketch to verify that they were the same man."

Prosecutor Ventura said, "Objection to this line of questioning. Señor Contreras is trying to trap the witness into admitting she was coerced into identifying Professor Villars as her assailant."

"Sustained," said the judge. "Señor Contreras, please phrase your questions so as not to be leading the witness." Pausing for effect, the judge continued, "Do you have any further questions for this witness?"

"No, Your Honor."

The judge then said, "Señorita Rios, you are excused. Prosecutor Ventura, please call your next witness."

Prosecutor Ventura stated, "I call Señora Paula Pazo Arrieta Gonzalo Ariel to the witness stand."

A middle-aged lady rose from her seat and walked with a purposeful stride up the aisle to the witness stand, and, taking her seat, she was sworn in.

Prosecutor Ventura asked her, "Is your residence in Madrid?"

"No sir. I live in Toledo with my husband and four children."

"Were you the victim of a rape?"

"No, but my twelve-year-old daughter was."

"Can we ask why you are here instead of your daughter?"

"Yes. She is underage and also because of the trauma to her, both physically and mentally, she was advised not to appear as a witness."

The Urge

"Do we have a photo of your daughter so we can see what she looks like, or were you advised not to show it to the court?"

"We were advised against it; but, after my daughter learned she could not appear in court, even though she is so young, she insisted I show her photo to the court. Her photo has been given to your court technician."

Turning from her for a moment, Prosecutor Ventura asked the technician to show a photo on the screen. The audience moaned in horror. The picture on the screen showed an extremely small and very pretty little girl with long dark hair and lustrous dark brown eyes.

Prosecutor Ventura then asked, "Señora Pazo, could you describe what happened to your daughter?"

"Yes, we ran out of bread." She started to cry and stopped talking.

"Please continue."

"It was all my fault. I'd forgotten to get enough bread for dinner, so my husband and I sent her to buy a loaf at the overnight deli." She sobbed. "The deli is only a block-and-a-half from our apartment. It should have taken no more than fifteen minutes, but when an hour passed, we called the police." She wiped the tears which were now coursing down her face.

Prosecutor Ventura said softly, "That's all right. Take your time."

After blowing her nose in her handkerchief, Señora Pazo continued, "The police found her quickly, but she was in shock and badly injured."

"Can you describe that further?" Asked Prosecutor Ventura.

Chapter 36

"He raped my virgin daughter. Her insides were ripped and bleeding. We had to take her to the hospital where she underwent surgery to repair what 'the animal' had done to her."

"Did she identify her rapist?"

"Yes. When she saw the photo of Franco, she screamed over and over again, 'That's him. Don't let him get me again.' She had to be sedated."

The courtroom erupted into a thunderous roar as everyone looked at the picture of the beautiful child on the screen, the distraught mother, and the man sitting at the defendant's table. Even after many loud raps on the gavel, the noise hardly abated. It was as if the hatred of rapists and the realization of the evil entailed had taken over the spectators. Everyone was angry. Finally, yelling at the top of his lungs, the judge exclaimed, "This courtroom WILL COME TO ORDER!" And - it did.

Prosecutor Ventura said, "Thank you, Señora Pazo. That will be all." The judge then asked, "Señor Contreras, do you wish to cross-examine this witness?"

"No, Your Honor, but I do wish to consult with my client. Could we ask for a brief recess?"

"So granted," said the judge. "This court will adjourn for a two-hour recess." He rapped his gavel and strode off to his chambers. Almost everyone in the courtroom rose to their feet and headed for the doors.

Señor Contreras and Professor Villars were escorted to a small room off the courtroom. After the door closed behind them, Señor Contreras said, "You animal! How could you? Everything and I mean everything, you've told me has been a lie. How can you continue to think I can get you acquitted from all these offenses? This

The Urge

last one is by far the worst. A child? I implore you to change your plea. Maybe, I can get you a plea bargain or somehow reduce your punishment if you do that. You might even plead insanity? What am I to do with you?"

Professor Villars said, "I'm not insane - I'm innocent. I can't control what I am. I'm not a rapist. I only follow my body's urge. I'm a victim."

"What?"

"Never mind. You'd never understand. I still say, I'm not guilty. I'll never change my plea."

Señor Contreras said, "OK. I must follow what my client's wishes are, but God help you when you're found guilty and given the maximum sentence."

~~

Chapter 37
Teresa Terrapiña Ruis Avila Zeroga

Officer Teresa Terrapiña had only been at the Madrid police station for five months. She had come directly from the police academy and had filled a needed spot in the computer section of the police department. With more and more information being compiled by the department, the computer section had increased significantly over the last five years, but it always seemed more computer specialists were needed. She had been a welcome addition.

Officer Terrapiña had scored very high in all the fields of study as a cadet in the academy, but her real expertise was computers. She was so good as to outrank several of the male cadets. There had been some friction when the male egos were aroused as scores had been compared. A few of the guys had been quite surly with her. While he didn't dislike men, in fact, she very much liked men, she believed women should be treated equally in the workplace. When she saw or heard men putting women down, she bristled.

Because computers were her forte, she had

The Urge

blossomed during her months on the job, especially in analyzing raw data and synthesizing the facts into documents. Her work had put a number of criminals behind bars. Her superiors were quite complementary both to her and behind her back. Some of them had privately bet that before too long she might be asked to head the computer section of the department, despite her age.

Several of the younger officers on the force became very good friends with her, particularly Detective Mendoza. He had just come running up to her desk and said, "Please drop whatever you've got going on right now. The trial of Villars had already begun for today and we think we could really send him away if we had some additional facts."

"Of course," Teresa said. "What do you need me to do?"

Handing her a thumb drive, he said, "This is a list of known rapes to have been committed by Villars."

She pushed it into her computer and watched as a list appeared before her on the screen.

Detective Mendoza said, "This list of rapes can be proven. You'll see two things. First, the rapes toward the bottom of the list are increasing in frequency. Second, there are some gaps in the list. We'd like you to do a quick search of our unsolved rape cases by date, especially in the gap areas of our known list. If you could, we'd like to see if the M.O. of some of our unsolved rape cases could be matched to our known cases. We'd also like, if you can, to make a third list dovetailing our known list with our unsolved list - maybe color-coding our unsolved ones so they stick out prominently. Oh, and one other thing - there was a girl who was not only raped but killed. Her name was Carmen Báez. She was a university student. I helped

Chapter 37

work that case. We'd like to prove he committed that one too."

"And, I'm assuming, you need all this during today's session?"

"If possible. Sorry to ask you to do this search so fast, but we just thought of this possibility before today's court convened."

"I'm not sure if I can do this or not, but I'll do the best I can. Are you going to wait, or should I call you when I have the information?"

"I'll wait. Hopefully, there will be a recess sometime this morning, but we can't count on that. I'd rather be here so I can take the information to the courtroom as soon as possible. But - if my presence will make you more anxious or slow you down, I'll leave, and you can call me."

"No, you can wait. Just don't talk to me. I'll work as fast as possible."

Detective Mendoza sat in a chair next to the office door while Officer Terrapiña attacked her computer keyboard.

Her fingers seemed to fly. Thinking quickly, she logically assumed she'd need the list of unsolved rapes first. After she had retrieved that list, she quickly scanned the list for Carmen Báez's name and placed an asterisk beside it. She color-coded the unknown list so that it would be different from the known list. She saved the unsolved list. Working on two different screens simultaneously, she laid two lists on top of each other. A comparison seemed to leap from her screen. The assumption Detective Mendoza had described to her was evident. The rapes, not all but most, in the unsolved list now filled in the gaps in the known list. Significantly, Carmen Báez's name was helping to fill

The Urge

in one of the gaps. Teresa saved the combined list. She took a blank thumb drive and copied the unsolved rape list and the combined unsolved-known list. She was glad she had color-coded the list and had placed the asterisk beside Carmen's name. He handed Detective Mendoza both thumb drives and begged him to stay for just a little while.

Officer Terrapiña, referring to the unsolved list, started a search of the M.O.'s of these crimes. This part of her search took the longest. She could see Detective Mendoza fidgeting in his chair, but her search was bearing fruit. If what she suspected was true, his wait would be worth it. She'd be able to supply everything he needed.

A half-hour passed. When she looked up, Detective Mendoza had disappeared. She continued working. An hour-and-a-half later when she looked up, having just hit the button to print her document showing the unsolved rapes followed the same M.O. as Villars', Detective Mendoza entered her office. He was back and he was carrying a file folder.

She said, "Here you are, Sir. It's all there. This should really help to put him away." She held out a printed sheet to him.

Detective Mendoza, who had been trying in the last week to work up enough courage to ask her for a date, said, "I really owe you one for this. Can I pay you back by taking you out to dinner tonight?"

Officer Terrapiña replied, "I'd really love that, but you don't need to do that."

He said, "Oh but I want to take you out."

She answered, "It's a date then. I'd love to go out with you."

~ ~

Chapter 38
The Trial Resumes

The trial was almost ready to convene. The spectators, jury, and prosecution had filed back into their seats. The judge hadn't made his appearance as yet, but the bailiff stood by the door for it to open for the judge. Villars and his defense attorney, Señor Contreras also hadn't come in from their lawyer-client meeting.

Detective Mendoza entered the courtroom and hurried down the aisle, making his way directly to Señor Ventura, Marielena, and Diego where they stood speaking quietly to each other next to the Prosecution table. He had both thumb drives, the printout of the MOs of the unsolved rapes, and his personal case folder. He quickly explained the evidence, giving both the thumb drives to Señor Ventura. Then he opened his case folder of the rape case involving Carmen Báez.

While Officer Terrapiña had been working on the computer analysis, he had gone into his office files on the Carmen Báez case. His file contained Carmen's photo, a printout of her physical size and weight, and the autopsy results. Carmen had been petite and around the age of many of Villars' victims.

At the very top of the victim rape information was the date of the night when the rape and murder had occurred. The rape had occurred, as he had remembered, on a weekday night in Madrid which also fit into the pattern of Professor Villars' rapes, with the ones on the weekends being outside Madrid and the weekday ones being in Madrid. He pointed out to them that everything fit nicely with Marielena's guess concerning the possibility that Villars had not only raped Carmen but also murdered her. Furthermore, several more gaps in Marielena's list of known rapes by Villars had now been filled by the unsolved rape cases.

Marielena asked, "Can we hook up your computer with all this data to the projection system in the courtroom? I need to be able to go back to the witness box and add this to today's testimony. By the way, thank your computer guru for us. Fantastic work!"

Prosecutor Ventura said, "Absolutely. I'll talk to our technician, and we'll have it ready when court adjourns again. I really think this will be our last hurrah. I think we will have presented as much against Villars as we can to get a guilty verdict."

Marielena said, "I think so too. I wonder if Villars will change his plea before we have to use this latest evidence."

"We'll soon know," said Prosecutor Ventura.

Diego turned to Marielena and said, "This latest idea of yours was pure genius. I wish I had thought of it."

"It just seemed logical," said Marielena demurely

Chapter 38

with a smile.

Everyone filed back into the courtroom and the judge said, "This courtroom is now back in session. Señor Contreras, have you had an opportunity to speak with your client, Professor Villars?"

"Yes, I have, Your Honor."

"Would you like to add or say anything?"

"No, Your Honor."

"Very well. Prosecutor Ventura, would you please continue your case against Professor Villars."

"Your Honor, I call again to the witness stand Detective Cortez-Rivera."

Marielena walked quickly to the Witness Stand and took her seat.

"I again remind you that you are under oath."

"Yes, Your Honor."

"I wonder if you could explain more about the alleged rape activities of Professor which you have discovered in your search?"

"If the technician could please show the first image, please," said Marielena. "Now, if the Jury would direct their attention to the chart of thirty rapes which we can directly tie to Professor Villars, both in the Madrid area and in other localities. As you can see, there are some things which will catch your eye. Both the rapes in and outside of Madrid show a pattern. First, rapes in the Madrid area occurred during the week. Second, rapes outside the Madrid area occurred on weekends. These facts lead me to surmise that our rapist lived in Madrid and raped Madrid women during the week. He vacationed elsewhere on weekends and raped there on weekends." She paused for effect, then added,

The Urge

"Professor Villars lives in Madrid and we understand from things he's shared with his colleagues and students, he had a habit of going outside Madrid for weekend vacations."

"You mentioned a third thing to me during the recess. What is that?" prompted Prosecutor Ventura.

"There are gaps in our known cases of rapes. However, when you look at the frequency of rapes, we do know that the frequency or time between rapes was becoming shorter and shorter."

"What does that tell us?"

"That Professor Villars' rapes were becoming more and more frequent over time. He was searching for more victims more quickly and committing rapes more often."

"Did this fact lead you to any conclusions?"

"Yes, Sir. On the police files list, there was a number, fourteen to be exact, of rapes for which we had no possible suspect, both in Madrid and other areas. We started to combine the two lists and they matched perfectly. Our cold-case rapes fit Professor Villars's pattern of rapes or the rapes which we could without a doubt assign to him, either because the victim identified a Franco mask and his physical attributes or for which we have conclusive DNA matching evidence. Please show the list when they are combined. Notice we took the liberty of using a different color to highlight the cold-case unknown assailant rapes. Also notice how the gaps in our first list have now been filled with highlighted second-color rapes. Note how the dates and frequency dovetail with my comment about the frequency of his rapes steadily increasing as well as where they occurred."

The audience looked closely at the projected image

Chapter 38

and whispered to each other as they concluded that the detective was indeed correct in her observations. Not only did the unsolved cold-case rapes fit perfectly into the known rape list, but the frequency WAS increasing.

Marielena and the Prosecutor waited until they knew the Jury and the whole courtroom of spectators saw what they wanted them to see.

The Prosecutor then asked, "Is there anything significant about those unsolved cases of rape?"

"Yes. I believe there is. The unsolved rape which has an asterisk beside it in the margin is particularly significant, we believe."

"How so?"

"That is the case of a Madrid university student who was raped on a weekday night. Please show the photograph of the victim which we obtained from her roommates." She paused for emphasis. "Carmen Báez was extremely petite. She was raped - and then - murdered only a block or so from her apartment."

The courtroom immediately came alive with voices and shouting causing the judge to rap his gavel for order.

"Please continue, Detective," said Prosecutor Ventura.

"If you look again at the chart, you'll see that her rape and murder fits, exactly, into a gap where we definitely know Professor Villars's rape list had a blank. We believe that it was Professor Villars who raped her because she also fits his choice of physical attributes of his victims. We also believe it was him because this was a time period when his rapes were increasing in frequency. While we can't prove it, we believe that

The Urge

Professor Villars is guilty of Señorita Báez's rape and murder; just as we believe that Professor Villars is guilty of all the many rapes, we have now linked to him. Although it is unusual for a serial rapist to kill his victim, we believe we have enough circumstantial evidence to add a charge of murder two, unpremeditated murder, to his list of crimes."

"Thank you, Detective Cortez-Rivera. I have no further questions."

The judge asked, "Señor Contreras, do you wish to cross-examine?"

Señor Contreras just sat and didn't respond, as if he were in a daze.

The judge again asked, "Señor Contreras, do you wish to cross-examine this witness?"

Señor Contreras stammered, "No. Your Honor."

"Prosecutor Ventura, do you wish to continue?"

"No, Your Honor. The Prosecution rests their case. May we remind the Jury to remember everything they have seen and heard and render the appropriate verdict when the time comes."

The judge addressed the courtroom, "This trial is adjourned until tomorrow morning at ten o'clock when the defense will be allowed to present their argument and witnesses for the defendant." He raped his gavel and the courtroom emptied. Professor Villars was escorted back to his cell while Señor Contreras continued to sit silently at the defendant's table.

~ ~

Chapter 39
Thought & Actions

Professor Villars was lost. He really had known it for a long time. It was like a dream - no, a nightmare. While outwardly he appeared calm and collected, inwardly he felt like he was wandering through a fog. It was a fog as dense as the fogs which had swept into his hometown of Bairritz off the cold coast of northern Spain in the winter and which were driven by bitingly sharp winds which bashed high waves against its cliffy shoreline.

He had always thought he'd never be caught. He'd been raping women practically all his life. No one, but a couple of professors, had even though he carried some dreadful secret in his makeup. Even then, he'd denied it. No, there was nothing wrong with him. He was fine. - No. There had been something wrong. The more he tried to convince himself he was OK, the more in his heart he knew he was different - and evil.

Now he was behind bars. Tomorrow his lawyer would be trying to defend him. He had so loved his freedom

The Urge

to come and go at will; to be considered refined and educated; to be asked his opinion of other's artworks; to be able to satisfy "the urge" whenever he chose, however he chose, and with whomever he chose. He couldn't choose anything now. He felt hemmed in - claustrophobic.

He was marched to eat, marched to shower, marched to see his lawyer, marched to recreation, marched to court and back, and marched yet back to his cell. His days were dictated to him, when to rise, when to eat, when to be left to his thoughts, and when to sleep. Bells, buzzers, and lights monitored his existence. If this trial ended as he now anticipated, the rest of his life would be a repeat of this last week, but even more intolerable because it would be unending. He wasn't sure he would be able to stand it.

The worst punishment he knew, even if they could prove the murder, which he knew they couldn't, would be life imprisonment. The rest of his life would be forever without hope of ever getting out or doing what he wanted to do. He had thought he had choices all his life, but he had made all his choices based upon "the urge".

He realized from the offhand and snide remarks of his fellow prisoners, whenever he walked by them in the hall, the shower, or the cafeteria that his life would be "hell on earth". One of the prisoners had said, "You know my sister was raped by a man like you. I know, she described it to me. We prisoners have talked and we're going to see how you like being raped. We'll find a way. By the time they carry you out of here, you're going to think you're a pin cushion."

Another prisoner said, "That poor little girl - man you're sick. But never mind, we'll get even for her."

Still another had said, "How in the world did you

Chapter 39

think you'd get out of all those rapes? Some of us in here deserve to be here, but you're worse than all of us. We're going to have some fun with you, 'dear Professor Denial'."

Still, another said, "I believe you'd rape the Virgin Mary herself. Don't worry. We'll be sure you'll never rape again - not our sisters, or our girlfriends, and definitely not our mothers."

He was scared.

Then there was the fact that he had a son. Never had he dreamed that the one rape then he'd not used a condom, was the one where his victim became pregnant. For his son to be a spitting image of himself was *just* punishment - not for the son and the mother - but for him. When he had looked at the young man, it had been like looking at himself.

Maybe, he had never really looked at himself and what he had become. There was no way though that he could deny siring that boy.

"I'm definitely far from being his parent."

He thought about all the young people, boys and girls alike, he had worked with and taught and nourished all those teaching years, there really was only one young person whom he should have nurtured and cared for - someone who obviously had needed him, but now loathed him so much he wouldn't even accept him for what he was - his father.

Yes, he hadn't gotten along with his parents, but his own father had at least tried to stick up for him.

What had he done? He'd run away - away from everything.

As he remembered that first rape, he realized he had taken advantage of a poor, unhappy girl who

The Urge

already had enough problems without his adding to them. Looking backward in time, he knew he could have found someone to have intercourse with who really wanted him. He'd found enough of those through the years. He discovered he'd been angry and hurt, rejected and distressed himself at the time. He'd taken his sexual "urge" and frustrations out on an innocent. He'd been doing the same thing for years. Too many years!

As the hours of the night slipped away, he came to a conclusion. The lights had gone out hours before. He reached up and pulled down the second blanket from the top bunk, but rather than covering himself to sleep, he started to tear both blankets into long strips. About an hour before dawn, he had woven all the strips into a long rope with a noose at one end.

He climbed up to the top bunk and firmly attached one end of the rope to the headboard. He played out the other end and slipped the noose over his neck. The length was perfect so that by the time he'd roll off the end of the bunk, the noose would tighten around his neck. He would refuse to fight, and it would be all over. He'd not have to deal with "the urge" and its consequences ever again.

He slid to the end of the bunk, tested the strength of the rope again, tested the noose around his neck, and rolled off the top bunk.

~ ~

Chapter 40
Day 5 of the Trial

The lights in the jail were turned to full. A new day was beginning. The speakers on the walls told the prisoners that in ten minutes they would be marched to the cafeteria for breakfast. The guards started walking down the aisles checking on the prisoners to see if they were in compliance with the instructions. When the guard in Professor Villars's aisle glanced into the cell, he couldn't believe his eyes. Professor Villars had hung himself from the upper bunk. His neck was obviously broken from its weird angle, his head and face were bloated and turning from red to black, his mouth was open, and his tongue protruded from his lips. His prison uniform pants were wet and stained from urine and feces. His last worldly offense upon his world.

The guard grabbed his phone and reported the death to his superiors. How could this have happened? Professor Villars had been the model prisoner. He hadn't even complained about the prison food. He'd been so polite and mild-mannered that all the guards

The Urge

had agreed that he was almost likable as a person, a far cry from their opinion of some of the other prisoners. His demeanor never had suggested that he was a risk, either to others or to himself. No one had even suggested he be put on a suicide watch. Supposedly today his lawyer was to be given a chance to clear him of all charges. All the guards had talked about how the trial was progressing. Well - there would be no trial today. The guard wondered what would happen next and was glad he wasn't in charge. He was also glad he'd just come on duty and hadn't had the night shift.

As the word spread to all concerned, the night guard was called in and asked if he'd checked on Professor Villars any time during the night. He said that he had walked by as the lights were ready to be dimmed and he had seen Professor Villars quietly lying on her bunk. It had appeared to him that the prisoner was getting ready to sleep, or in fact, might already be asleep. His back had been turned toward the cell door and he couldn't see his face. He hadn't heard any noises at all from his station at the other end of the aisle, but that station was as far removed from Professor Villars's cell as possible. He also had not been summoned by any of the other prisoners who might have heard or seen anything. With the prison cell doors staggered along the aisle, no one could have been able to see into Professor Villars's cell from their cell. No one could have seen him tear the blankets into strips, weave them, or use them to make a rope. No one could have seen his jump off the top bunk - or his demise. After the questioning, he was allowed to assume his normal duties. It looked as though the professor had waited until he could work quietly and then commit suicide.

The Prosecutor alerted the defense attorney that his client had committed suicide. Señor Contreras in shock asked, "Wasn't he on suicide watch?"

Chapter 40

"No. We had no idea he was in such a state as to assume we needed to. Did you have any idea?"

"No. The last words we had were during yesterday's trial. He told me he thought the character witnesses we had lined up for today were enough, and he still proclaimed his innocence."

"Was that before or after the end of yesterday's testimony about the unsolved cases matching gaps in cases known to have been done by him?"

"Mmmmm - it was before."

"Did you speak to him after yesterday's session?"

"No. I think I was in shock. The fact that he might also have been a murderer was almost too much to absorb. I believe I was still sitting at the defense table when he was led off to go back to his cell. I said nothing to him, and he said nothing to me. I couldn't believe that I would have to defend him with only a few character witnesses. I was completely overwhelmed."

"I can sympathize. We had enough evidence that a few friends couldn't be enough to save him. At least now you won't even have to try." The two men shook hands and parted.

The Prosecutor, Madrid police department members who had been involved in the case, Marielena, and Diego met to draft a press release concerning Professor Villars's suicide. They ended up writing a very terse statement which not only told of his death but also stated the obvious - there would be no day five for his trial. While his victims would not see Professor Villars pay for his crimes, his victims could be sure that Professor Villars would no longer be raping the women of Spain.

As they finished Marielena said, "This suicide

The Urge

proves two more things about Professor Villars."

"What?" They all asked.

"Number one, it proves how good an actor he really was. He completely fooled all of us with his mild manner and politeness; just like he fooled all of Spain about his being a rapist."

"What else?"

"I think he proved that he really did have a conscience. He couldn't live with what he had done."

"Maybe so," they said as they all stood to leave their meeting room.

~ ~

Epilogue

As Diego and Marielena drove back to San Anton from Madrid, they were silent for the better part of the journey.

At last, Diego spoke. "You know the professor would have been found guilty either today or in a few days when the trial ended?"

"Yes, I know," said Marielena.

"You know something in addition to that, I hope?"

"What?"

"You conducted one of the finest police investigations I've ever been privy to. You solved these crimes almost by yourself. I hope you can see that."

"I had lots of help from you and the other police departments, especially the Madrid department; from Señora Oso in the library, as we traced rapes all over Spain; from the victims themselves, so that I could sketch from their descriptions what the rapist looked like; and from the forensic computer technician who helped with those lists and their specialized software."

"Yes, but it was you who put it all together. Plus, you did it at the same time as mastering self-defense with master Chow and painting the awesome mural at city hall. I'm so proud of you."

"You're only saying that because you love me."

"That I do", he said as he smiled broadly.

~ ~

Elaine C. Wolfe

Retired educator and artist, Dr. Elaine Wolfe, accomplished one of her bucket-list goals in 2020 when she published <u>The Spanish Beauty.</u> She returns to Spain for her second mystery, <u>The Urge</u>, with some new twists involving her same beloved characters. Dr. Wolfe combines her story-telling abilities, developed during 36 years of teaching biology, with her lifetime experiences as a professional artist, and her love of Spanish culture.

Dr. Wolfe has traveled to every continent except Antarctica, has been recognized nationally for her teaching abilities, and has been recognized as an award-winning professional artist. She has been, for over forty years, and continues to be an artist-owner of the CCA Art Gallery in Carmel, IN.

Dr. Wolfe is the published author of her 400-page dissertation, science articles in "The American Biology Teacher" and "The Hoosier Science Teacher", and poems in The National Library of Poetry's "Best Poems of 1998" and "Whispers at Dusk". She is a Distinguished Purdue University Alumna in the School of Science.

www.ingramcontent.com/pod-product-compliance
Lightning Source LLC
LaVergne TN
LVHW021232080526
838199LV00088B/4321